NEW GIRL

I opened the class door and stood there while everyone turned to see who'd come in.

"Well?" the ugly teacher asked. Miss Lear herself, no doubt. "Who are you?"

"Erin Whitney." I thrust the papers toward her.

She wouldn't take them. Her neck had turned red. "Whitney? You're a Whitney? Are you related to Amelia?"

"She's my cousin," I said.

"Hey, Erin, sit here beside me," a voice called out from the back of the room.

"Don't sit next to Nicholas," Miss Lear said. "You haven't been admitted to this class yet."

I waved the papers over my head. "Remember these?"

"I said, you haven't been admitted yet."

Ah, I thought. A game-player. Let's see what you do when you run into somebody who won't play. Poor Miss Lear. She had a lot to learn about battling somebody who didn't have anything to lose . . .

Other Avon Flare Books by
Jean Thesman

COULDN'T I START OVER?
THE LAST APRIL DANCERS
WAS IT SOMETHING I SAID?
WHO SAID LIFE IS FAIR?

THE WHITNEY COUSINS Trilogy
AMELIA
ERIN
HEATHER

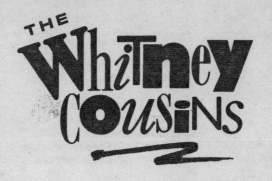

THE WHITNEY COUSINS

ERIN

JEAN THESMAN

AN AVON FLARE BOOK

THE WHITNEY COUSINS: ERIN is an original publication of Avon Books. This work has never before appeared in book form.

AVON BOOKS
A division of
The Hearst Corporation
105 Madison Avenue
New York, New York 10016

Copyright © 1990 by Jean Thesman
Published by arrangement with the author
Library of Congress Catalog Card Number: 89-91538
ISBN: 0-380-75875-X
RL: 4.8

First Avon Flare Printing: May 1990

AVON FLARE TRADEMARK REG. U.S. PAT. OFF. AND IN OTHER COUNTRIES, MARCA REGISTRADA, HECHO EN U.S.A.

Printed in the U.S.A.

RA 10 9 8 7 6 5 4 3 2 1

Chapter 1

I think my shadow is growing smaller. Someday
it will run away or vanish, and then I'll really
be alone.

                                        The Castaway

My uncle Jock Whitney came for me at my grandparents' house in Oregon shortly after noon on a Sunday in March. He was much as I'd remembered him
from six years before when I was ten—big and rum-
pled, with shaggy brown hair and the bright green
Whitney eyes. And laugh wrinkles. My grandparents
only had frown wrinkles.

"Well, Erin," Uncle Jock said when he saw me,
"you grew up when I wasn't looking."

Grandma Burns sniffed. "If she grew up, then the
rest of us missed it." Grandpa nodded. I could tell
he wanted to add something, but Uncle Jock wasn't
giving him a chance.

"I'll take Erin's things out to the car now," Uncle
Jock said. "We've got to be on our way if we want to
make good time to Seattle. Sorry we have to rush off."

Grandma Burns frowned at me. "Erin, don't ruin
things for yourself again. You're running out of places
to live."

I didn't answer her. What was the point? I picked
up my bag of shoes and followed Uncle Jock out to
his car.

1

"What's in this box I'm carrying, lead?" he asked, laughing.

"Books," I said. "There's another box of books inside, too. I'll carry it."

"Didn't I see *two* more boxes stacked in the hall? Are both of those yours?"

"The other is full of art materials, but they aren't too heavy," I said. "I'll bring it out." I was mindful that what Grandma Burns had said was true. I was running out of places to live, and suddenly I was scared. If I made Uncle Jock angry—and I had a knack for making everybody angry—then I might just end up where Grandma and Grandpa said I would—in a foster home.

I scurried back to the house with Uncle Jock. "I can carry everything," I said. "You wait in the car."

"Heck, no," he said. "When we get around to your clothes, I expect that'll be the biggest job of all. I know it would be with your cousin Amelia."

He lugged out the other box of books and I carried the box of art supplies, with my portfolio stacked on top. We went back and I picked up my bag of clothes.

"That's it?" he said, incredulous. "Your clothes are in that plastic bag?"

Grandma sniffed again. "A trash bag for the trash. I don't want you thinking that we didn't get her decent clothes. Lord knows we tried again and again to teach her to dress properly, but she ruined everything we gave her and wore those old rags instead, so finally I said to her grandfather, 'Art,' I said, 'it's no use. She wants to look like one of those bums down on Front Street, so let her. I wash my hands of her.' That's what I said."

Uncle Jock glanced at me, then back at her. "She looks fine to me," he said, but I knew he was lying.

2

I didn't even look fine to *me*. I looked absolutely weird, the way I intended looking.

We all stood around awkwardly for a moment. That should have been the time for fond farewells, but nobody was fond of anybody else, so finally I mumbled something about being grateful (after all, they were my mother's parents), told them I'd be in touch (a flat lie), and said good-bye. They didn't walk out on the porch with us. They didn't even look out a window.

When Uncle Jock started the car, he gave a big sigh of relief, causing me to burst out laughing.

"You sure look like a Whitney," he told me.

That was the best thing he could have said, and I'm sure he knew that.

On the long drive to Seattle, he told me about my cousins. Amelia was my age and a sophomore. After Amelia came Jamie, who was ten. I remembered him as a funny little preschooler who was always into mischief. Then came two little girls I'd never met, six-year-old Cassie and Mimi, who was five.

"They're a handful," Uncle Jock said. "You'll have to be patient with them. They ask too many questions and eavesdrop when you're talking on the phone. And they're messy. Your aunt Ellen says you can dress them up but you can't take them anyplace. They'll love that hat you're wearing, so you'd better hang on to it."

I pulled my felt hat down a little farther and grinned.

"If you don't mind my asking," he went on, "where did you find the hat? My father had one like that. He called it a fedora."

"I got it at the same thrift shop where I got the rest of my clothes," I told him, and I watched his face closely to see how he'd react to that.

He looked straight ahead at the freeway unrolling ahead of us. "Thrift shop," he said. "I hope you'll tell Amelia about that, because every time she heads off for the mall, I keep checking my pulse to see if I'm healthy enough to face the bills.''

We rode in companionable silence for a while. Then he said, ''I don't believe I know another girl who wears her hair in a long braid like yours. It looks nice. Your father loved your hair—it's the same color your grandmother Whitney's was. He was glad that one of the grandchildren had that nice, reddish-brown, thick hair.''

My fists automatically clenched in my lap. I didn't want to talk about my father—or my mother. I leaned my head back and closed my eyes, hoping he'd take the hint. He did. He didn't talk again for an hour.

At last we pulled up in front of a big, rambling old house in Seattle, one I remembered clearly from my childhood. Once I'd lived only a few blocks away. As soon as the car stopped, my cousin Amelia ran out on the porch, smiling, waving, and trying to hang on to the collars of two big, shaggy dogs.

''Oh, look at you!'' she said when I got out of the car. ''What a great hat! And your hair! You must be able to sit on it.'' She didn't mention my clothes, I noticed.

She let go of the dogs, who barked at me, jumped on Uncle Jock, and then jumped all over me. I knelt to hug them. When I looked up, four more people were coming out the door.

Aunt Ellen. I recognized her, although she was heavier and her hair was turning gray. Jamie looked like a taller version of what he'd been.

''That's a great coat,'' he said. ''Where'd you get it, the Army surplus store?''

''Tell you later,'' I said. Two little girls eyed me, grinning.

''Are you Erin?'' the one with glasses said. ''I'm Cassie and this is Mimi.''

4

The younger one grinned. "Can I have your hat?"

"Mimi!" Aunt Ellen said. "Come inside, Erin. It's starting to rain. I've held dinner for you, so let's eat first and catch up on the news later."

News. What in particular did she want to hear about? That I'd been expelled from school for painting a mural on the wall in permanent paint outside my algebra class? I was sure she already knew that.

"I'm awfully tired," I said, "and I'm not very hungry. If you could just show me where I'm supposed to sleep, I think I'll lie down."

Everyone was silent for a moment, and then Aunt Ellen said quickly, "Of course. I'm being thoughtless. You came a long way and you must be exhausted. You take a nap, and later, if you're hungry, I'll fix you whatever you want."

A cup of poison was what I wanted, but I didn't say that. Amelia led the way upstairs to her bedroom, which I'd be sharing. I brought along the bag of clothes and Uncle Jock carried up the boxes.

"I've cleared out half my closet for you," Amelia said, opening the door to show me.

"I don't use hangers," I said, and I tossed my bag of clothes on the closet floor, then dropped my bag of shoes on top of it. "This is good enough for me."

Amelia didn't say anything. When I stole a glance at her, I saw that her face was red. Well, too bad, I thought. We might as well get things straight right away. If she thinks I'm going to spend hours and hours fussing over clothes and makeup the way she probably does, then she'd better think again.

They left me alone, so I washed up, got into my nightgown, and went to bed. I pretended to sleep for hours, until they all gave up on me. Long after everyone else was asleep, one of the dogs came in and crawled up on the bed with me, snuggling close. I put my arms around her and cried quietly into her fur. Here you go again, Erin, I thought.

The next day Amelia walked to school with me, ticking off various bits of information she thought I should know. When I signed up for classes, she said, try to avoid getting a Miss Lear, who was a monster. The art teacher was wonderful. Ask for the same lunch break Amelia and her friends had. I only half-listened. None of that mattered.

When we got close to school, there were other kids on the sidewalk, too, kids who stared at both of us. A few said hello to Amelia. About a block away from school, two girls caught up with us and asked me if I remembered them. I wasn't sure, but I said no, just to be on the safe side. I didn't know what they wanted yet.

"Don't you remember me? I'm Wendy Ingram," the dark-haired girl said.

"I'm Meg MacArthur," the one with light-brown hair told me. "Remember? Everybody called me Moochie in grade school."

I shrugged and didn't smile. There was no point in pretending that I wanted to be friends. Friends ask questions.

They were careful not to look at my clothes very long—I was wearing my hat, of course, and a long, denim duster over an ankle-length black skirt and huge, baggy purple sweatshirt. My shoes were canvas high-tops, well-worn so they had character. The other girls looked like every other high school kid in the country.

Amelia walked me to the office, and I told her I'd take it from there. I handed over my transfer papers and waited while the woman behind the counter made out a schedule for me. Bells rang, kids hurried in and out (always staring at me), and finally I got my schedule.

"You'll be late to first period so here's an admission slip," the clerk said.

6

I thanked her and went out into the empty halls to search for the room. English was the class. I looked closer at the schedule. Miss Lear was the teacher, the monster Amelia warned me about. So what, I thought. Most teachers were monsters.

I opened the class door and stood there while everyone turned to see who'd come in. There were stares and a couple of snickers.

"Well?" the ugly teacher asked. Miss Lear herself, no doubt.

Might as well start out on the wrong foot, I thought. "Well what?" I responded.

She scowled. If that was the best she could do, I thought, she was in big trouble. I waited for her to say something else. She simply stared at me. I waited. She waited. Somebody began laughing.

"Are you coming in or not?" Miss Lear asked.

I shrugged and came in. When I held out my admission slip and the registration schedule which she was supposed to sign, she said, "What are these?"

"Beats me," I said. "They're for you, but if you don't want them, I don't care."

"Who are you?"

"Erin Whitney." I thrust the papers toward her.

She still wouldn't take them. Her neck had turned red. "Whitney? You're a Whitney? Are you related to Amelia?"

"She's my cousin," I said.

Miss Lear sighed. "I should have known from that getup of yours. I suppose you're one of the clowns, too."

I looked down at my clothes. "Nope," I said. "I dress like this because I'm poor and weird."

The class erupted into laughter and the red in Miss Lear's neck spread to her face.

7

"Hey, Erin, sit here beside me," a voice called out from the back of the room.

A boy who seemed to be much younger than everyone else in class beckoned to me. He wore glasses, braces, and a sweatshirt like mine, only more faded.

"Don't sit next to Nicholas," Miss Lear said.

"I don't mind." I sat down beside the boy.

"You haven't been admitted to this class yet," Miss Lear said.

I waved the papers over my head. "Remember these?"

"I said, you haven't been admitted yet."

Ah, I thought. A game-player. Let's see what you do when you run into somebody who won't play. "Okay," I said, and I got up and left.

Poor Miss Lear, I thought as I strolled out of school laughing. She had a lot to learn about battling somebody who didn't have anything left to lose.

I didn't go home. Instead, I took a Metro bus downtown to see the city I'd left when I was ten years old. So much had changed. There were more tall buildings, more traffic, more people. I walked through the Pike Place Market, skipped down the stairs to the waterfront, and when I'd satisfied myself with the view, I took a bus north to the zoo.

There was much that was new and wonderful there. The sun came out around three and the school-age kids showed up, replacing the mamas and babies who'd been there earlier. I found a bench in the Elephant Forest and settled down. In one deep pocket I carried a small sketch pad. In another, I had pencils, a couple of felt-tip pens, and a candy bar. What more could anybody want?

The elephant closest to me had eyelashes several inches long. She was poking under a log with her trunk, feeling around for something. Frustrated, she

8

curled the end of her trunk into a fist and hammered on the log. I laughed aloud.

"Hey, I know you."

I hadn't noticed two boys standing nearby until one of them spoke. I shielded my eyes from the afternoon sun and studied him. Did I know him? Maybe.

"You're the girl who won the state art contest when we were in grade school. Erin Whitney. I'm Brady Harris, remember? I was a year ahead of you."

He was tall, with rough, curly brown hair and nice hazel eyes. I still didn't recognize him with certainty—I had a way of blocking out everything that happened before I was ten—but I nodded to him anyway.

"This is Carl MacArthur," Brady said. "He goes with Wendy Ingram. Remember her?"

"I met her again this morning," I said.

"You were at school?" Brady asked, astonished.

Carl nudged him. He looked uncomfortable. Then to me, he said, "You scared Wendy and Amelia. They were looking all over for you. Then they heard about you and Miss Lear."

I scowled down at my drawing. "It's an awfully big school for gossip to pass around that fast."

"Well, you're hardly going to go unnoticed, not in that outfit," Carl said, laughing. "Why the costume?"

I looked up from under the brim of my hat. Carl looked interested—but Brady looked embarrassed. He suspected that I was in my own clothes—and I had an eerie feeling that he might even know why I'd chosen them—something I wasn't too sure of myself.

I stuffed my sketch pad and pencils away as I stood up. "See you around," I said and I walked away swiftly, my long skirt flapping around my ankles.

That Brady. I'd have to keep away from him.

9

Chapter 2

_____

If school counselors cured everybody's problems, they wouldn't have jobs anymore. Pretty
scary, if you think about it.

                                        The Castaway

When I got home, I learned that Amelia had explained my cutting school to Aunt Ellen and Uncle
Jock by telling them that Miss Lear had been "cruel"
to me.

Interesting. I'd had teachers who were worse. But
my aunt and uncle were sympathetic, saying, "Amelia
has problems with that woman all the time," and
"You can't let her discourage you."

"I can take care of myself," I said. "Honestly."

My younger cousins, the ones called "the little
guys," caught on, though. I was alone with them in
the living room for awhile before dinner, and Jamie
said, "You gave Old Lady Lear a hard time, didn't
you?"

"How'd you guess?" I said as I flipped through
TV channels, looking for a cartoon program.

Jamie grinned. "You look like somebody who's
cool."

"What's cool?" Mimi demanded. "I want that."

Jamie laughed and told me about an incident at
Mimi's kindergarten, when the teacher wouldn't let
her leave the room to go to the bathroom and Mimi

walked out, heading straight for the principal's office, where she threatened to call the police.

"Way to go, Mimi," I said. I loved these kids.

Mimi sat on one side of me and Cassie curled up on the other side. "What's it like being an orphan?" Cassie asked.

I glared down at her and saw her serious eyes behind the glasses, so I erased my scowl and did my best to smile. "You don't want to try it," I told her. "Trust me on this."

Jamie poked Cassie's leg. "You aren't supposed to ask questions like that."

"It's okay," I said. "As long as it's you guys. But I don't let other people ask me anything."

"I'm going to be like that, too," Cassie said.

"Yeah. Sure." Jamie snickered. "You tell everybody everything."

Aunt Ellen interrupted the argument by announcing dinner. Nothing more was said about my running off that day—but the next morning, Aunt Ellen told me that if I had trouble again with Miss Lear, I was to telephone home immediately.

"We want the school to understand that we're intensely interested in what happens to you," she said. "Amelia's had problems and we try to stay on top of everything. But we can't unless you keep us informed. Amelia had to learn that the hard way."

I nodded, but I had no intention of calling home or anyplace else over Miss Lear. And if Amelia had learned something the hard way, well, she shouldn't have been surprised. What other way was there of learning things?

It's not that I didn't like my cousin. But she was no kid anymore, not like the little guys.

The school morning began the way I knew it would. I got to first period before Miss Lear, took a seat next to the kid with glasses and braces—Nicholas Brown was his name—and pulled out my sketch pad. While I waited for class to start, I drew animals. Nicholas hung over me, breathing on my neck, saying, "Great! Oh, that's great. Wait until Mrs. Nugent sees what you can do."

Miss Lear came in. The class became so silent that you could actually hear somebody chewing his fingernails.

"Who are you?" Miss Lear asked, looking at me.

"Sorry about your short-term memory problems," I said calmly. "Let's try it one more time. I'm Erin Whitney, Amelia's cousin. And I dress this way because I want to."

Somebody besides Nicholas laughed aloud.

"You're not officially in this class," Miss Lear said.

Same game, second inning. I shrugged. "I had a registration slip yesterday but I don't know what happened to it," I lied. It was in my pocket.

"You left the class yesterday without permission," Miss Lear said.

"Since I wasn't officially in the class, I didn't think it mattered what I did," I said. I smiled unhelpfully. "Shall I leave again?"

"Oh, you're so *bad*," Nicholas whispered, grinning.

"Go to the office," Miss Lear said.

"Why not?" I said. I gathered up my sketch book and pencils and slouched toward the door.

"I won't put up with this," Miss Lear cried suddenly.

I smiled as I walked out, leaving the door open behind me. Moments later I heard the door bang shut.

At the office, I talked to a woman called Mrs. Camp, explaining that I couldn't seem to get *in* Miss

Lear's class and now had been thrown out, even though I wasn't exactly in—if she saw what I meant.

She looked me up and down, smiling a little. "I love the hat, but the sweater puzzles me. Where did you find one that says Prison Farm on it?"

I told her about the thrift shop. "You can buy sealed cartons of stuff for seven dollars a pound, and you have to take what you get. The possibilities are wonderful."

"I can see that," Mrs. Camp said. "Well, I'll have to send you in to Mr. Depard, who's the sophomore counselor, and I should warn you in advance that the sweater may be off-putting. What are you wearing underneath?"

I unbuttoned the long, baggy sweater to display a tee shirt that said, "You're too fat and your mother dresses you funny."

"I'd leave the sweater buttoned if I were you," she said, sighing faintly. "Follow me and take off your hat. Please."

I didn't take off my hat, but I buttoned up the sweater.

Mr. Depard was bent over tying his shoes. When I walked in, he sat up, gawking.

"I'm Erin Whitney," I said, and I added, "Amelia's cousin."

"Oh, lord," he muttered to himself. He leaned forward, propping himself on his folded arms. "What's wrong?"

I explained that I couldn't get in Miss Lear's class and why.

He wasn't listening. "Are you part of that clown troupe?" he asked. "I've explained to Amelia, Wendy, and Meg that they can't go on disrupting their schooling because of their outside jobs."

"These are my clothes, not a costume," I said.

13

"If you don't like them, don't look at them." I unbuttoned my sweater. He blinked and sucked in his stomach automatically. It always worked.

He babbled forever, on and on and on, repeating all the stuff I'd heard for years. When he stopped for breath, I said, "Are we done talking yet?"

He didn't say another word. Instead, red-faced, he wrote me out another admission slip for Miss Lear's class and shoved it across the desk to me. I walked out—and I left the door open.

As I passed Mrs. Camp, she said, "You have beautiful hair. Do you always wear a braid?"

I nodded and flashed a smile at her—as I heard Mr. Depard's door slam. The noise was music to my ears. I didn't bother returning to Miss Lear's room, but waited in the john until the bell rang.

In my art class I found Nicholas Brown again, sitting in the back, and I took the stool next to him.

"Well, at least you didn't lapse into a coma," he said.

"What?" I asked.

"You went to Depard's office, right?" he said. "I doze off in there, honestly. And in some of my classes, too. I think I'm coming down with narcolepsy."

"What's narcolepsy?" I asked. What a weird kid.

"It's the opposite of insomnia," he told me. "It's when you fall asleep without any warning during the day."

"Wish I had it," I muttered.

He poked my arm in a friendly way. "You'll like this class. No kidding. Mrs. Nugent is actually a real person, not a 'noid."

I gaped at him. "What's a 'noid?"

"A humanoid, a humanoid," he cried impatiently.

"How old are you, anyway?" I asked.

14

"Fourteen. How old are you?"

"Almost sixteen," I said. "You sure don't look fourteen."

"It's all in the genes," he said. "You should see my mother."

I studied him for a moment, then asked, "You're a genius, aren't you?"

"Jeez, no," he said indignantly. His thin little face flared red. "Can I help it if I like to read?"

I shook my head. "I like to read, too, but you're different. Really, really different."

"Yeah," he said with satisfaction. "Where'd you get the neat sweater?"

I explained again about the thrift shop in Oregon, and he told me he knew where one was in Seattle that also sold stuff by the pound. "We could go there after school someday," he said.

The bell had rung long before and I saw the teacher walking up and down the aisles, checking work. She'd seen me, but she didn't leap on me, demanding paperwork, explanations, and apologies. By the time she reached our table, I'd borrowed a sheet of paper from Nicholas and sketched out what I remembered of the swamp and marsh exhibit at the zoo.

"Hmm," Mrs. Nugent said when she saw it. "I like that. What's your name?"

I told her, and before I could identify myself as Amelia's cousin, she said, "I recognize Amelia's green eyes. Welcome to class. I see you've met the resident pest?"

"Who, me?" Nicholas exclaimed, genuinely outraged.

"Oh, there's one in every class," Mrs. Nugent said, smiling as she walked away.

During lunch break, I didn't intend sitting with my cousin and her friends, but they were saving a place for me at their table, so I didn't have a choice—not without seeming even ruder than I usually was. I went through the cafeteria line, trying to pick something that wouldn't cause me to die prematurely. All the food came in flimsy plastic cartons and packages, and it looked exactly like leftover airline food.

"Did Air Transylvania sell this to you or did they just drop it off as they flew over, like a load of bombs?" I asked a cranky-looking woman behind the counter.

"Are you a student here?" she demanded. "I don't recognize you."

"I'm from the Board of Health," I said as I paid the cashier. "They do research on me instead of animals. If I throw up within an hour, you're dead meat—and probably the main course tomorrow."

The kids in line laughed, but the woman only scowled and muttered.

"What happened in line?" Amelia asked when I got to her table.

"Nothing much," I said. "I was only commenting on the looks of the food and she took it personally, I guess."

"It is awful," Amelia said. "We used to have cooks—a real kitchen, you know. Now this comes from somewhere else—nobody knows for sure."

"They get it out of the dumpsters behind the jail," Wendy said.

"They fish it out of the water behind the ferries," Meg offered.

Two boys came over, sitting farther down the table. One I recognized—Carl MacArthur. He'd been with Brady at the zoo. Amelia introduced the other—Mark Reid—and I could tell they were crazy about each other.

"Great hat," Mark said. "Are you interested in

16

working with our clown troupe? We're getting so much business that we could use help.''

"Try it,'' Amelia urged. "You'd have so much fun with us. And you'd earn tons of money, too. We're practically getting rich.''

I shook my head as I unwrapped what probably was supposed to be a sandwich. "I'm not an actor and I don't want to be.'' I didn't add that I didn't need money. One thing about being an orphan, you never need money. You get an allowance from a lawyer's office and money for clothes and everything else you could ever want. If you want anything. The rest of it sits there in banks, waiting for you to grow up. It's supposed to make you feel better because you don't have parents, only photo albums that you can't bear to look inside.

Suddenly I was angry. Really angry, like I got sometimes, when I couldn't see any color but red and my head buzzed as if I had a million bees zipping around between my ears, stinging and stinging.

I threw the horrible sandwich down, picked up the tray, and started for the cashier. "I want my money back!'' I cried. "I'm not going to pay for stuff like this! At my house, we wouldn't even feed it to the dogs; we'd scrape it straight into the garbage can!''

I had everybody's attention, and that was all right. What's a tantrum for, if nobody listens?

The cashier only stared, but the woman behind the counter yipped something about turning me in. I slapped my tray down and held out my hand to the cashier.

"I want my money,'' I said.

"Don't you give her anything!'' the woman behind the counter yelled.

The cashier shrugged helplessly. "Could you,

maybe, choose something else you might like better?'' she asked me.

"No, no!'' the woman cried. "No exchanges. That's ridiculous.''

My anger dried up. I wasn't hungry, anyway. There were other ways of dealing with the situation. I left my tray where it was and went back to the table.

"Did you get your money?'' Meg asked.

I shook my head. "But I'm not done with them yet. Nobody should have to pay for food that bad.''

"It's been bad all year,'' Wendy said. "Maybe we ought to have a food strike.''

We would have explored that idea, but someone interrupted us. A girl leaned over me, smiling, but her smile wasn't real. "I heard about you,'' she said. "Everybody heard about you.''

"Go away, Fritzie,'' Amelia said.

The girl didn't leave. "You're making more enemies than friends, you know,'' she told me. "Especially after the way you've treated Miss Lear.''

"Who *are* you?'' I demanded.

"Fritzie Seton,'' she said. "I'm a friend of Amelia's.''

Amelia snorted and laughed. Obviously Fritzie was dreaming.

I decided to give this Fritzie Seton a hard time. "*Who* did you say you were?'' I asked.

"Fritzie Seton,'' she said, annoyed now.

I looked her up and down. "Good grief,'' I said. "What a burden.''

And then, before anybody said anything else, I got up and strolled out of the cafeteria.

I could see that it would take awhile to break everybody in. I didn't like to be messed with.

I was on my way to my locker when Brady Harris

18

stopped me. "I'm glad to see you're sticking it out today," he said.

"The day's not over yet."

He grinned. "I was going to call you tonight. Carl and I are giving Mark a surprise birthday party. Not even Amelia knows about it yet. I'd sure like it if you came."

"I never go to parties," I said, and I walked away.

He followed. "What do you mean, you never go?"

I shook my head angrily and ducked into the girls' john.

The last party I went to started out fine, but the ending turned out to be the end of everything. I was ten. I went to a birthday party for Patty Murphy. When the party was over, everybody else's parents came to get them. Mine didn't, because they were dead. They died in a car crash while I was standing out on the Murphy's porch waiting for them.

I never went to another party. Hey, who knows what else might happen, right? Maybe I only thought that losing my parents was the most horrible thing. Maybe God or Fate or whoever's running things could actually come up with something worse.

Me, I didn't take chances.

Chapter 3

I don't understand why people put up with things they hate. You can't change anything unless you complain. Of course, nothing may change anyway, but at least you had the satisfaction of scattering around a little misery where it's most deserved. I mean, why should the jerks in the world be happy?

The Castaway

During lunch break on Wednesday, I found mold on my sandwich. I'd already eaten half of it.

Mark, Amelia's boyfriend, saw me staring at my sandwich, leaned closer, got a good view of the mold, and said, "See, Amelia? I told you the sandwiches are left over from last summer."

"Yuck," Wendy said.

"Throw it away," Amelia told me.

"Stomp on it," Meg said. "It might have something alive in it."

"Write a letter to the school paper and complain," Carl said. "You remember Brady? Sure you do. He's the general news editor."

"He's also junior class president and advisor to the student council and . . ." Mark said.

"So?" I interrupted.

"You'd be surprised how much he can get done," Mark said.

"So why hasn't he complained about the food himself?" I asked.

"I don't think he knows how bad it is," Wendy said. "He goes home for lunch. He fixes hot food for his little sister."

"His mom died last year," Mark said. "So he picks Jannie up at kindergarten every day, feeds her, and drops her off at the day-care center."

I wrapped up my sandwich. "He's a solid gold hero, right?"

Amelia poked me. "Hey, he really is, Erin. Everybody says he's going to be president someday."

I sighed. "Okay. He's perfect. Meanwhile, I'm hungry and I won't buy anything else here. I can't figure out why anybody does!"

"Tell Brady to run an article on the food," Carl said.

"Write a letter about it," Mark urged.

"Draw a picture of it!" Amelia said, laughing.

"I don't do cartoons," I said as I got up from the table. "Excuse me, folks. I've got a complaint to make."

I carried the moldy sandwich back to the cafeteria and showed it to the woman behind the counter. "This time I want my money back. Tell the cashier, or I'm going to take this up to the office and show it to the principal, and then take it home for my family to see."

A crowd gathered around to gape at the sandwich. The kids who were in line left it and stampeded the vending machines.

"She ought to get double her money back," a girl standing next to me said. "There's stuff at Bailey's Antique Store that's younger than that sandwich."

The woman nodded to the cashier, who returned my money. The girl who'd been talking to me followed me out of the cafeteria. "Where are you going now?" she asked.

Her hair was tinted three different colors and she wore four earrings in one ear. Her sweater was too tight.

"Who are you?" I asked.

"Val Guthrie," she said. "I saw you in the cafeteria yesterday. You're new, aren't you? Where are you from?"

"Oregon."

"Why did you move here?"

"I was thrown out of school there."

She thought that over and it seemed to meet with her approval. "So what's your name?"

"Erin Whitney."

"Are you related to Amelia?"

"I'm her cousin."

She pranced alongside me without saying anything for a moment. "Aren't you going to eat lunch?" she asked finally.

"I'm going across the street and around the corner to that grocery store and buy something." I glanced sideways at her. "Are you coming?"

She nodded and shrugged at the same time. "I get stuff there once in a while. They've got little packages of cheese and crackers. But they won't let you eat in there."

"That's all right. I like taking walks during lunch break."

A group of boys standing around the school door called her by name, and she grinned and waved at them. Not a single girl we passed acknowledged seeing her.

We bought cheese and crackers at the store and circled the block a few times, eating and exchanging comments about the weather—nice for March in Seattle—and TV programs—neither of us watched much.

"You want a blind date Friday night?" she asked. "I know this guy from another school, and he's got a friend . . ."

"Forget it," I said.

"But . . ."

"No."

"You got other plans?" she asked.

Friday was the night that Mark's friends were giving him a surprise party, but I wasn't going to that, either. "I have to baby-sit my little cousins," I lied.

"We could come to your place," she offered quickly. "As soon as we get the kids to bed, we can party."

"No," I said. "It's not that kind of place."

She snickered. "Every house is that kind of place if you put your mind to it."

I stared her down. "No partying at my house. I don't party. Not ever."

Now it was Val's turn to stare. "Why not?"

"None of your business," I said. "Look, isn't it time to get back to school?"

"I do as I please," she said, and I believed her. I did as I pleased, too, but I was sure that the things that pleased us were very different.

She strutted off in the direction of the Metro bus stop and I went back to school, just in time for my history class. I sat in back, next to a football player who called himself Bub. The teacher called him Elroy.

Yesterday Bub had taken one look at me and decided that I'd probably never be the woman for him. Today, on second sight, he was sure of it.

"Why do you dress so weird?" he asked me. He wasn't smiling.

23

"Why is your neck so thick?" I asked in return. "Is it because your head is solid rock and weighs a ton?"

Our interest in each other, not great to start with, dropped to zero after that exchange. I listened to the teacher, drew pictures in my notebook, and sighed with relief when the class was over. The only thing I had on my mind was Carl's and Mark's suggestion that I write to the school paper about the cafeteria food. It sounded like a fun project. But I wasn't certain I wanted Brady Harris, everybody's hero, involved in my life.

Well, what was wrong with an anonymous letter?

The paper might not print it. Then again, maybe it might.

That evening, I wrote and rewrote a letter, explaining that I had to remain anonymous because I was afraid of retribution, but something had to be done about the food before a student was actually poisoned by it. "School is bad enough," I said, "but is the cafeteria food some sort of punishment that we're also expected to pay for?" I signed my letter, The Castaway.

I was working at the desk in the family room and heard the phone ringing, but I didn't answer it. A moment later Amelia called out that someone wanted to speak to me. She sounded, well, almost annoyed. Or embarrassed. I couldn't decide.

I picked up the phone and recognized Val Guthrie's voice. "You want to go out for hamburgers? A couple of guys came by my house and they'd like to meet you."

Was she crazy? Nobody ever actually *wanted* to meet me. "I'm busy," I said. Amelia was standing in the doorway, watching, so I added, "But thanks for asking me."

After Val hung up, Amelia edged into the room as if she was bringing bad news.

"What's up?" I asked.

"Erin—well, I'm sorry Val called you. You're new—no, not exactly new, but Val didn't go to grade school here so you don't know what she's like."

"You aren't making a whole lot of sense," I said. I tried to smile, but I had to wonder where this conversation would end up.

Amelia came in and sat down next to the desk. "She has an awful reputation. And she doesn't really like other girls, she only uses them. I don't think you want to get mixed up with her. Maybe she hasn't done everything the kids say she has, but still, she's not your sort. Not at all."

"How do you know what sort I am?" I asked.

Amelia's face turned red. "You're sure making this hard."

I picked up my letter and pretended to reread it. "I hate it when kids gang up on somebody."

Amelia was silent for a long time. I looked up.

"I know everything there is to know about being ganged up on," she said. She looked upset. "And that's not what I'm talking about. Val is always in trouble—everywhere. She seems to like it. It's as if trouble excites her. She's very manipulative, and she doesn't have any friends."

"You mean she doesn't have any *girl* friends," I said. "All the boys seem to like her."

"You noticed," Amelia said flatly.

"I also noticed that you don't have as many girl friends as you used to," I said. "So maybe you ought to feel sorry for Val instead of shutting her out."

Amelia bit her lip. I could tell she was furious. "Okay, you're right. I do feel sort of sorry for her. But I'm not going to get involved with her because I don't want to have the kind of trouble she's got. I've got enough of my own.''

She'd already hinted that something was wrong in her life, but she didn't tell me anything more, and I didn't ask. I'd had enough experience myself with nosy people, so I always backed away unless somebody volunteered to tell me their secrets.

"Truce," I said, and I raised my hands. "Don't worry about me. I can handle Val." I grinned at her. "You've got to admit that I won't be attracting the usual sort of pals around school."

Amelia burst out laughing. "Whose fault is that? You're so ferocious!"

"I need lots of space," I said, and that time I went back to the letter and didn't look up again. Amelia took the hint and left me alone. That was all the little-girl confidences I planned on exchanging with her for the rest of our lives. She had problems—I had problems. All God's children had problems.

The next morning I shoved my letter in the slot in the school paper's door, trusting that somebody would find it and read it. Nobody saw me and I walked away, pleased with myself. Brady wouldn't suspect that I was the Castaway.

I'd brought a sandwich from home that day and planned on spending lunch break alone, walking around the school neighborhood. But rain started falling at eleven, so I ended up at Amelia's table. Everybody there had brought food from home.

"You've started a revolution," Carl told me.

"Not me," I said. "Consider me a permanent by-stander."

I wondered what they'd think if my letter appeared in the paper. Of course, I'd deny writing it.

In history that afternoon, Bub (who was not slated for a career as a brain surgeon) tried to cheat on our

26

test. He took a dozen paper scraps from his pockets, and he held them in his lap, searching through them for answers.

I hate cheating. I hate people who cheat. I watched him out of the corner of my eye for a few minutes, and then I made a big show of pulling off my cardigan, looking for a place to put it, and finally accidentally on purpose dropping it over his arms. In the scramble, I managed to knock a lot of his paper scraps on the floor.

"Oh, gee, I knocked your notes on the floor," I said. "How awful. Shall I help you pick them up?"

The history teacher was quite interested in this disruption and called Bub to his desk. Meanwhile, I finished the test and drew pictures on the back of it. Bub left the room, banging the door.

After class, a boy said, "Bub gets real mad when people make trouble."

"So do I," I answered. "And since I'm smarter than good old Bub, I can make more trouble."

The rain had ended at lunchtime so after school I stopped in a small park near the house to sketch squirrels. The trees were beginning to leaf out, and the air smelled like spring. After a while I took off my hat to let the sun shine on me.

"I thought I recognized you," Brady Harris said.

I looked up and saw him with a little girl who had curly hair like his. But she was more interested in my hair.

"Is that real?" she said, pointing to my braid.

"Sure. I haven't cut it since I was ten. I'm Erin. Who are you?"

"I'm Jannie."

Brady sat down next to me. "It turned out to be such a nice day, I thought I'd pick Jannie up from

27

day-care early and take her for a walk," he said. "We saw you and decided to stop and say hello."

Jannie seemed curious about my sketch pad so I handed it to her. She showed it to her brother. "Look at the squirrels."

Brady studied the drawing for a while. "You're really good, Erin."

I didn't respond. Instead, I took the pad back and did a quick sketch of Jannie, tore out the sheet, and handed it to her as I got to my feet.

"Take it, Jannie. Next time I see you here, I'll show you how to draw a squirrel," I told her.

"Hey, where are you going?" Brady called—but I'd already put some distance between us and didn't look back.

Jannie had sad eyes, just like the ones that I used to see whenever I looked in a mirror.

Chapter 4

I never could figure out why schools hire teachers who hate kids. It's like hiring an ax murderer to take out your appendix.

The Castaway

Aunt Ellen and Uncle Jock were good to me—but they tiptoed around me as if I were a bomb about to go off. I could imagine what my grandparents had told them about me—everything I'd actually done and a lot of things they'd only thought I'd been doing. I hadn't gotten along at the school in Oregon—not ever. I didn't have any friends. And I spent all the time I could alone in parks or libraries or just wandering downtown streets. I didn't see any particular reason to change any of that after I moved back to Seattle.

But my relatives saw things differently. The whole family was accustomed to doing things together, and naturally they thought I'd want to be included. I didn't have anything against them—but I didn't want to deal with them all day long on weekends. At least, not in one big mob.

"Won't you come with us this morning?" Cassie asked me during breakfast that Saturday morning. Everybody but me was going to watch Amelia and her friends do their clown act at a supermarket opening.

"I've got too much homework," I said. I put on my most helpless expression and looked at my aunt.

"Changing schools isn't as easy as I thought it would be."

I could see that Aunt Ellen was disappointed, but she nodded and told me she understood.

"Can't you put it off?" Jamie begged.

"Yes, can't you?" Amelia asked. "I'll give you all the help I can when we get back. I'm anxious for you to see us in action. And maybe someday you'll do a skit with us."

I had to laugh at that. "I can imagine how much the other clowns would enjoy that."

"They really like you," she said. "Honestly. You've got such a goofy sense of humor. And Mark said that Brady was asking all sorts of questions about you, so we think he's going to ask you out. He was sorry you didn't go to the birthday party for Mark last night."

I put down the toast I'd been nibbling on. "What sort of questions was he asking?"

"Oh, you know," she said, suddenly evasive.

"Like how come I'm living here instead of with my own parents?"

She nodded. "Well, he already knew that. . . ."

"That they were dead," I finished.

Cassie sucked in her breath and Mimi choked on her juice.

"It's okay, gang," I said. "You don't have to pretend that it didn't happen. Now, what did Mark ask, Amelia?"

"He wanted to know if you had a boyfriend in Oregon, and if you missed the boy and all that."

"What did you say?"

"I told him I didn't know—because I don't," Amelia said. "Did you?"

"Maybe she doesn't want to talk about it in front of everybody, including the dogs," Jamie said indignantly.

Uncle Jock laughed then. "I don't blame her," he said. "The dogs gossip all around the block. Come on, gang, let's put our plates in the dishwasher and get ready to leave. I want places right in front this time."

He saved me again—Uncle Jock was diplomatic. But the little guys hung around after everybody else went off for their coats.

"Did you have a boyfriend?" Cassie asked.

"Did you?" Mimi echoed.

"Aw, leave her alone," Jamie complained. "Of course she didn't have a boyfriend. That's disgusting."

"Right," I said. I didn't add that nobody had ever asked me for a date. Let's get real, kids, I thought. Who'd take a bag lady anywhere?

But don't get me wrong. That didn't bother me. From what I'd seen of dating, somebody always got hurt. And remember me? I'm the girl who didn't take chances.

They finally left, the little guys and my aunt and uncle in one car, and Amelia in the van that showed up for her while she was still shaking wrinkles out of her costume for a character called Tiny Tina, the fattest clown I'd ever seen.

As soon as they were out of sight, the dogs and I went back to bed. I hadn't been sleeping very well, and it was catching up to me. We didn't get up until late afternoon.

On Sunday, Amelia went off with the clowns to a little kid's birthday party, my aunt and uncle took Jamie to a basketball game, and I baby-sat the girls and the dogs. We made fudge and I showed them how to draw each other. It was the nicest Sunday I'd spent in a long time.

And then Monday came. Monday and Miss Lear— and the school paper.

Things might have gone a lot better if Miss Lear hadn't decided to read poetry aloud. I like poetry, and I hate hearing people read it out loud because they hardly ever do it right. Miss Lear did it worse than I'd ever heard, and the poem was one she'd written herself. Ugh.

"Don't laugh, whatever you do," Nicholas whispered. He'd seen me biting my lips until my eyes watered.

But his warning came too late. I tried to swallow my laugh, but it came out like a bark, which made Nicholas giggle.

Miss Lear stopped reading. "Am I correct in thinking that you don't care for poetry, Erin?"

I shrugged, hoping she wouldn't force me to answer.

"Well?" she asked. "Weren't you taught to reply when someone speaks to you?"

"Since you *insist,*" I said, "that stuff you were reading wasn't exactly Shakespeare."

"You're dead," Nicholas groaned.

"And you're an expert on Shakespeare, are you?" Miss Lear asked. Her smile was small and tight, and her little eyes glinted.

"No, but I've read some of the plays and the sonnets."

"Is that so?" she asked. "Suppose you share a bit of Shakespeare with us right now."

"Oh, no," Nicholas whispered. "You're not lucky enough to be dead."

I sat up straight. " 'For I have sworn thee fair and thought thee bright, who art as black as hell, as dark as night.' "

There was a short silence, and then everyone laughed.

Miss Lear's face turned a nice shade of purple. "Erin, you aren't half as clever as you think you are."

" 'What? wouldst thou have a serpent sting thee twice?' " I said. I was so angry that I could feel my heart beat in my throat.

"To the office," she croaked.

I settled my hat squarely on my head and marched off. "What the heck," I said as I passed her desk. "I've been thrown out of better classes than this one. 'Cry "Havoc!" and let slip the dogs of war.' " Out in the hall, I could hear the kids laughing until Miss Lear slammed her door.

Mr. Depard told me I had an attitude problem. It showed in my speech, my expression, and my behavior. How's that for a news flash?

"Look at you," he said. "You wear peculiar clothes to deliberately provoke people. That hat—it's ridiculous. How do you suppose your aunt and uncle feel about your dressing that way? Don't you ever think of anyone but yourself?"

"No," I said.

He hadn't expected that answer. "Well—well, you should."

"Okay."

He rattled some papers on his desk. "I have a report from your last school."

I shrugged.

He leaned forward and smiled at me, startling me for a moment until I realized that the smile had been hastily stuck on, for effect. "You know, Erin, people really want to like you."

"Are we done talking yet?" I asked.

His right eyelid twitched. "Someday you'll look back on this . . ."

"Your shoelace is untied," I said. I got up and went to the door. And left it open behind me.

The school paper came out just before lunch break. I took one out of the bin in the main hall and saw my letter on the front page. For a few seconds, I had spots in front of my eyes so big that I couldn't read. That was the first time I'd ever seen anything of mine in print.

The letter opened an article written by Brady. Apparently he'd done some quick research and discovered that while he'd been eating real food in his own kitchen, the rest of us had been gagging to death in the cafeteria. According to his article, he wanted to know what had happened to the school kitchen. Everybody, he wrote, hated the packaged food brought in from somewhere else.

All the kids in the cafeteria had a copy of the paper, including the cashier, who was reading it and laughing when I walked in. I had folded mine up and shoved it in one of my big pockets.

"What's new?" I asked innocently as I sat down at Amelia's table and unwrapped my sandwich from home.

"As if you didn't know," Mark said. He plopped his paper down in front of me. "Don't try to tell us that you didn't write this letter."

"Me?" I asked. "Do I look like somebody who'd write to a school paper, for Pete's sake?"

"If it wasn't Erin," Wendy said, "I have a hunch it was the weird little kid—what's his name? Nicholas Brown. He's in my math class. The letter sounds like something he'd do."

"He doesn't eat in the cafeteria," Carl said. "His mother comes every day and takes him to a health food restaurant."

Wendy slumped over her homemade pizza. "Darn. Well, it sure wasn't me. Not that I haven't had those thoughts and worse. But I forgot all about it, what

34

with Mark's birthday and all." She eyed me. "Are you sure it wasn't you?"

I held my hat over my heart. "Give me a break."

But Mark's eyes were full of laughter, although he didn't say a word, not even to Amelia. As long as he kept his mouth shut, I was home free.

Nicholas caught up with me between classes, though, and waved the paper under my nose. "It had to be you," he said. "You're the only one in school besides me who could spell poison right."

That night Amelia read the letter to the family at dinner, and Uncle Jock laughed until he had tears in his eyes. "That's what so great about a free press," he said. "Now let's see what happens."

"I wish you'd told me how bad things were in the cafeteria," Aunt Ellen said to Amelia.

Amelia shook her head. "The food was never good, but usually I could swallow it. But lately it's been getting worse, and the other day Erin actually had mold on her sandwich. That was the end for most of us. Mark told me that Brady—he's the general editor on the paper—is taking it up with the student council Wednesday and presenting a request for a hearing with the principal the next day."

Mimi's eyes were round. "Is that the same as curating an incident?"

"Curating a what?" Uncle Jock asked.

Mimi spoke slowly and patiently to her father. *"Cu-rating an incident.* That's what my teacher said I did when I went to the principal because she wouldn't let me go to the bathroom."

"Creating an incident!" Jamie cried. *"Creating!* Are we going to hear about your bathroom problems for the rest of our lives?"

Cassie smacked her fist in his mashed potatoes.

"There. That's *creating* an incident. You can just stuff it in your ear."

"Mom!" Jamie shouted.

"Mom!" Cassie mimicked.

"Oh, lord," Uncle Jock said, raising his gaze to the ceiling.

I grinned. This was lots more fun than eating with my grandparents. And thanks to the little guys, everybody forgot about the letter in the paper.

The next morning before school, Brady stopped me as I was walking past his locker. "Did you see the paper yesterday?" he asked.

"Sure," I said. "Everybody's talking about your great article."

"Everybody's wondering who wrote the letter, too," he said. "I asked around. Nicholas Brown told me that there are only two people in school who can spell poison and he's one of them and he didn't write the letter. Somehow I couldn't help wondering about you."

"Me?" I asked. "Do I look like somebody who wants to be famous and get a letter published in the paper?"

He leaned close to me and straightened my hat. "No, but you look like somebody who gets involved sideways instead of head-on."

"What does that mean?" I said, pushing his hands away from my hat.

"I'm not exactly sure," he said, "but I like it. A lot. Jannie's been asking about you. When are you going to give her that drawing lesson?"

"Someday," I said vaguely, and I walked on without looking back. I was smiling and it didn't feel right. I mashed my hat down on my head and stomped around a corner.

Miss Lear was waiting for me that day. "I'm not

going to allow that hat in class any longer,'' she said when I came in.

I stopped in my tracks. "Now what's wrong? I haven't even sat down yet."

"You create stress in the class," she said. "I've talked to Mr. Depard about you. He agrees with me. You cause too much stress."

I shoved my hands in my pockets. "This room is already full of stress. All I did was stir it around a little."

"The hat goes," she said.

"I'll go with it."

And I left school again without permission. Some days you just can't help lucking out.

I caught the Metro to Woodland Park and visited the marsh and swamp exhibits. The wild grasses were growing there, and ducks paddled in the ponds. A mallard posed for me, bobbing on the water only three feet away.

At noon I went downtown again to the Pike Place Market, and I walked past all the farmers' stalls and up and down the narrow hallways, visiting one level after another. At last I stepped out to the long flight of stairs that led down to the waterfront, and found an artist there, working on a watercolor. I stopped to watch.

The man didn't look at me, but after a long time he said, "Aren't you supposed to be in school?"

"Aren't you supposed to be at work?" I asked.

"Smart-ass," he said, laughing. "You're an artist, am I right?"

I pulled out my sketch book and handed it to him. He paged through it quickly, then went back over it again, slower that time.

"Very good. Lots of animals, no people," he said.

I pointed to his painting. "And there's a street scene. Lots of buildings, no people."

"Takes one to catch one," he said. "Have you had lunch yet?"

"No. I'm going home now." That wasn't true, but it sounded as if I had plans.

"Wait a bit. Eat with me. We'll talk about animals and art and books."

I trusted him, which was unusual for me. He took me to a little restaurant crowded into a corner of the market, and we ate fish and chips and drank root beer. And we talked about ourselves. His wife had died. I told him about my parents.

"Do you ever find yourself looking for them?" he asked. "I catch myself watching for my wife in crowds, as if she'd gotten away from me somehow, and if I'm quick enough I'll be able to see her once more before she slips away for good."

He astonished me. I didn't think anybody else in the world did that. "Once I thought I did see them," I said. "When I was still a kid. It was Christmas and my grandparents took me to a big department store. I thought Mama and Dad were ahead of us, in the crowd going toward the escalator. I tried to catch up. But they were gone. Always gone."

"Always gone," he echoed.

I finished my lunch and thanked him, then walked up the hill to my bus stop. I remembered then that the man hadn't told me his name and I hadn't given him mine. He was the only one I'd ever spoken to willingly about my parents.

The next day at school, after I endured another lecture from Mr. Depard about cutting classes, I found Brady and told him that I'd meet him and Jannie someday after school in the same park where I'd seen them before and give his sister her drawing lesson. I had a hunch that sometimes she might find herself looking for her mother in crowds.

38

Chapter 5

Sometimes I can't see any point in trying. If I take one step forward, I fall off the dock.

The Castaway

When it came to actually making plans with Brady for Jannie's drawing lesson, I couldn't do it. A couple of times at school he made a point of finding me to ask if we could meet that day after school, and each time I told him I was busy.

Val was with me once. "Wow," she said when Brady left, mingling with the crowd in the hall. "Since when do you know Brady Harris?"

"Since I was a little kid," I said. That wasn't quite true. I didn't have any clear memories of my life before the day my parents died. Brady didn't even figure in those. But I didn't want Val getting any ideas about Brady and me. I wouldn't have put it past her to want to double date—me and Brady, along with her and one of the creepy boys she hung around with during and after school. The thought of it made me feel sick.

But one day after school when I'd taken Cassie and Mimi to the park near home, Brady showed up with Jannie, and as it turned out, Mimi and Jannie were friends from the same kindergarten class.

"I don't suppose this is the right time for a drawing lesson," Brady said as he sat down next to me.

I watched the little girls climbing the ladder to the slide. "I don't think she'd be interested."

"You come here a lot, don't you?" he asked. He wasn't looking at me, but instead he was watching sea gulls circling overhead.

"Yes. I feed the squirrels. Some of them know me now."

"Jannie and I came here every day last year," he said quietly. "After Mom died. We sat on this bench and watched the other kids play. After a while she started playing with them again, the way she did before when Mom brought her."

I refused to be drawn into the conversation. I had no intention, ever, of comparing notes with him about how it is to lose your mother.

But he wouldn't let go of it. "Sometimes I still can't seem to get past it," he said. "Sometimes I'm mad at the whole world. I think a lot of dumb things, things I hate myself for—like how could she do it? Leave me to take care of Jannie, I mean."

"You've got a father," I said angrily.

"Sure. But he works all day. And Jannie hates baby-sitters. She got left with them a lot when Mom was in the hospital. Things are better if I take care of her on the days she doesn't go to the day-care center. She doesn't much like that either."

I turned up the collar of my old Navy jacket and yanked my hat down a little farther over my ears. I didn't want to hear this.

He still wasn't looking at me. His gaze followed the lazy circles of the sea gulls. "I remember what happened to your parents," he said.

"I don't want to talk about it," I said, louder than I'd intended. The little girls stopped playing and stared at me.

"Sorry," Brady said hastily. He reached out and

touched my arm. "I'm really sorry. I don't know what got into me. I guess it's because of the day. This would have been my mother's birthday, and I keep thinking about her. Like I said, sometimes I can't seem to get past it."

"Well, I got past everything just fine," I said. I jumped up and called my cousins, telling them that we had to go home. They obeyed me, but unwillingly. Jannie said good-bye to me over and over, but Brady only said it once. From the dismayed expression on his face, I thought that he meant for it to be permanent.

I didn't talk all the way home, and when I got there, I found Wendy and Meg giggling with Amelia in the room we shared, painting their faces with clown makeup.

I gathered up my books and went down to the family room to start my homework. Mark, Carl, and Brad Willis, who was Meg's boyfriend, came in a few minutes later. Brad wasn't part of the clown troupe, but he was going along to watch the performance that afternoon, and he asked me if I wanted to go, too.

I shook my head and didn't look up from my history book. They all left, laughing and hurrying, and the front door banged behind them.

A hard knot of anger grew and grew in my chest, until it hurt to breathe. I slammed my book shut and sat staring at the wall for a long time. Suddenly I got up, took my jacket from the closet, and left the house without saying good-bye to anybody.

It was dinner time. As I walked, I saw people through the windows of their houses sitting at tables. Families.

Dark clouds blew across the sky, and after a while a light, cold rain fell. I caught a bus and rode downtown, then caught another and traveled north, then

41

transferred east. At the end of the line, I paid another fare and went back the way I came. The bus driver stared at me in his mirror for a long time. From the corner of my eye, I watched him watching me. I wasn't crying. I wasn't anywhere near crying. But my face was so stiff it hurt.

After a while I ran out of buses and money, so I walked. I was miles from home, but the rain had stopped, so I didn't mind. Nobody bothered me—nobody ever bothers people who look like they're crazy. I learned that a long time ago.

When I got home it was after eleven, and Aunt Ellen and Uncle Jock were waiting for me in the living room. The minute I got inside, my cousins yelled down from upstairs to see if it was me, if I was all right, and could they come down, too. My uncle told them to go back to bed. Only Amelia stayed at the head of the stairs. Her face was a pale oval in the dark.

"Are you really all right?" she asked. "Did anything happen?"

"I'm fine," I said, annoyed. What did she think I was, a kid? I was plenty old enough to be out after dark.

"Erin, come into the living room and sit down," Uncle Jock said. He looked up the stairs at Amelia. "It's all right, Amelia. Go back to bed now."

I clumped after him, sighing a lot, letting him know that he was wasting his time and mine, too.

After I sat down, as far away from him and Aunt Ellen as possible, he said, "You knew the rules. You're never to leave this house without telling someone where you're going. You're never to be alone after dark. And you're always to be home by nine-thirty on a school night."

"Okay," I said. "Can I go now?"

"Stay where you are," Uncle Jock said sharply. "You don't think much of our rules, do you?"

I shrugged. What was the point of arguing?

"Even rules can't keep children as safe as we'd like them to be," Aunt Ellen said.

"So why have them?" I asked.

"Because they're a start," she said.

They had prepared a speech. I knew all the signs. They weren't going to let me go until I'd heard it, so I leaned back and resigned myself. What I heard was a surprise.

"A few months ago," Aunt Ellen said, "Amelia went out with a boy who tried to rape her."

"Oh," I said, feeling as if my breath had been knocked out.

"She escaped from him, but she had to walk a long way home in the dark, through a bad neighborhood. She was lucky that nothing else happened to her." Aunt Ellen paused for a moment and blinked.

"There's more to the story," she went on. "The boy goes to your school, and he harassed her for a long time. He ruined her reputation with lies. She suffered a lot—and the rest of us suffered, too."

"This isn't a safe world, Erin," Uncle Jock said. "If you've gone this long, running around at night by yourself without finding yourself in trouble, then you're terribly lucky. We don't want your luck to run out. You don't need Amelia's experience—or anything worse. You are absolutely forbidden to leave this house without telling us where you're going. And you will never again leave it alone after dark."

I looked away from him, shrugged, and finally nodded.

"Erin," he said sharply.

I glanced back at him.

"I had two brothers. Both are dead. Your cousin

Heather never knew her father, but you knew yours. You understand loss and grief. I don't want to lose you or grieve over you. And so, like it or not, you'll follow our rules."

I raised my chin. "Heather's dad died because he was sick. My dad was killed in an accident. They aren't dead because they broke rules!"

"Rule are a start, and that's where *you* start," Uncle Jock said.

"You may go up to your room now," Aunt Ellen said. She sounded as if she was trying hard not to cry.

I went up. The light was still on in the bedroom, and Amelia raised herself up and jerked her extra pillow under her head when I came in.

"Did you get the Bottom Line Blow-up, or did they just chew you around the edges?" she asked. Her smile was a little shaky.

"I think it was the Blow-up," I said. I tossed my hat on the chair in the corner and pulled the elastic off the end of my braid, shaking out my hair. "You've heard it all, I guess."

"Oh, gee, at least a dozen times." Amelia examined her fingernails, pretending to be casual. "I heard them tell you about Warren."

"Was that the guy's name?" I asked. I undressed and tugged my nightshirt over my head, then sat down with my brush and began pulling it through my hair.

"I'll point him out to you at school next time I see him when you're with me."

"I can live without it," I said.

"You ought to know," she said stubbornly. "I should have told you before. I thought about warning you. . . ."

"But you decided that somebody who looks like me isn't likely to be bothered by the school rapist."

44

She laughed. "No, although you do have a point. He probably won't ever bother you because you act like you could take care of yourself. We heard about when you knocked out that boy's tooth—the boy who stole your wallet."

I grinned and kept brushing.

"I guess I didn't tell you about Warren because it's such a hard thing to talk about," Amelia said. "When I finally told my friends and the other kids at school, not everybody believed me. It was awful. Some people thought I'd brought it on myself. And Warren kept lying about me—telling kids—and Mr. Depard—that I was chasing him and calling him up all the time because I wanted to go out with him again."

I snorted. "Yeah, sure. What girl wouldn't want a second date with a prince like that?"

We both laughed suddenly. "Prince," Amelia repeated. "A million girls could kiss that toad and he'd still be a toad."

I put down my brush and crawled under my blankets. "Does he bother you now?" I asked.

Amelia clicked off the lamp on the table between us. "Nope. I embarrassed him one day during the clown act—he wishes he'd never met me. I think he's always afraid I'll start in on him again. Maybe I'm not good with my fists like you, but when my mouth gets in gear, I can be pretty dangerous."

"It's the Whitney curse, my grandmother told me," I said. "She thinks all the Whitneys are sharp-tongued and nasty."

"And green-eyed," Amelia added.

"Maybe one leads to the other," I suggested, grinning in the dark.

Amelia was silent for a moment. "Anyway, maybe now you understand how bent out of shape my folks were when you didn't come home or call or anything.

45

Dad even phoned Brady—I told him that Brady was a special friend of yours—and Brady went to the park to look for you and called back to say you weren't there. He was worried, too.''

I sighed, exasperated. ''I wish Uncle Jock hadn't done that.''

''Don't you like Brady?''

''Good night,'' I said. ''I'm tired and I don't want to talk anymore.''

I couldn't sleep—again. Sometimes it seemed to me that I went nights and nights without rest. After a while I heard Amelia's soft, even breathing, and knew she didn't have to deal with her thoughts for the rest of the night. Lucky her.

But then, a couple of hours later, Amelia cried out in her sleep, softly and pitifully. I sat up, staring at her in the dark.

Suddenly she cried out again and woke herself up.

''What's wrong?'' I asked.

I heard her flop down and turn restlessly. ''Sorry I woke you. Sometimes I have nightmares.''

Who doesn't, I thought.

''Erin?'' she whispered after a while.

''Yes?''

''You won't go out again after dark all by yourself, will you?''

I laughed a little. ''No. I promise. And I won't go out with Warren, either. Now can you sleep?''

''Yes,'' she said.

Silence again for a while.

''Erin?'' Amelia asked.

''What?'' I asked wearily.

''Why do you wear those clothes?'' she asked.

''Because,'' I said. I closed my eyes and turned on my side.

''For a while,'' Amelia said, ''after that night with

46

Warren, I used to think I was safe inside my Tiny Tina costume. I was invisible, sort of. Do you know what I mean?''

My eyes snapped open and my heart beat hard, thumping under my ribs. But I said, ''No, Amelia, I don't know what you mean. I'm going to sleep now. Good night.''

But I didn't sleep until the sky outside my window turned pale and the first birds sang.

Chapter 6

If I can't get away with anything, why should anybody else? Get real, world. Don't ask me to take care of you.

The Castaway

Spring arrived. The park was full of blooming trees and shrubs, and the new grass smelled sweet. I put away my hideous winter wardrobe and replaced it with my hideous spring clothes. I didn't have much, so Nicholas and I went to his favorite thrift shop, called First Pick.

He was looking particularly weird that afternoon. His socks didn't match, and for pants he wore the bottom of an old baseball uniform. His ancient black sweatshirt bore a drawing of a nuclear explosion. I, impeccably clad, wore a long flowered skirt, a sleeveless gray sweatshirt over a faded yellow shirt, and my summer hat, a sort of sailor's cap, white, turned inside-out.

The silver-haired woman who owned First Pick smiled when we walked in. "Nick, old son, I see you made use of the sweatshirt."

"Naturally," Nicholas said. "Mrs. George, this is Erin Whitney."

She studied me carefully. "I believe I know your designer," she said.

"Same as yours," I said. She wore a long, shape-

48

less gray dress and an equally shapeless tan sweater with the elbows out. And high-topped tennis shoes. There were at least four strands of glass beads tangled around her neck, and her earrings were made of macaroni painted with nail polish.

The shop was full of stuff that had been dumped in bins, not sorted out into sizes or colors or any other system I recognized. "How do we know where to start looking?" I asked Nicholas.

"You don't," he said, burrowing into the nearest bin. "If you see something that might fit either of us, pull it out. Then, when we've got a big enough pile, we'll bargain. She always starts out at a buck a piece, but we'll work her around to selling it by the pound. I usually pay six, sometimes five if the stuff is really awful." He hauled out a long pink nightgown with a ragged hem. "Interested?"

I shook my head. "I've got two like it." I started in on the bin next to his.

In an hour each of us had a pile that came to our waists. We rejected a lot of each other's choices, and finally settled on a stack of clothes for him and a slightly bigger stack for me. I'd been especially pleased to find a long, floating dress of fragile pink material with a handkerchief hem and a shawl with roses embroidered on it. The outfit would be too romantic without something to set it off—and I'd found just the thing—an oversized jacket with *Kip's Karate Klub* stenciled on the back.

"Oh, nice, nice," Nicholas rhapsodized. "Brady Harris will swoon when he sees you in that get-up."

"Never mind Brady," I told him, nudging him in his skinny ribs. "Miss Lear is going to leap with joy when she sees you in the knickers."

He held up the knickers. "How old do you suppose

49

they are?" he said, his eyes shining. "Maybe fifty years? Look at the holes!"

"Wear something substantial underneath or you won't have any secrets left from anybody," I advised.

We started the bargaining process. Mrs. George, even as she argued for a dollar a garment, dusted off a rusty old scale. "For you darlings only," she said.

"You lie," Nicholas said disrespectfully. "I happen to know personally two winos in Pioneer Square who told me you sell them stuff by the pound, and cheaper than you sell it to me."

"Their fathers aren't doctors," Mrs. George said. "Have a little pity, Nick." She stuffed his clothes in a plastic trash bag and plopped in on the scale. "Fifteen dollars even."

Nick pulled a handful of dollar bills out of his pocket. "This is all I've got, take it or leave it."

She snatched up the wrinkled bills. "Little thief," she grumbled. She eyed me next. "I suppose you're a poor orphan."

Nicholas burst out laughing, then sobered instantly. "Of course not," I said, pretending to be indignant. "My father is the chief of police." I handed her a ten dollar bill and thirteen cents. "That's all I've got except for my bus fare."

She sighed. "There's no point in weighing yours, then," she said.

"Not if you want me for a regular customer," I said.

"You drive hard bargains, both of you," she said as she shoved my stuff into another trash bag. "Now. How about a soft drink and some chocolate chip cookies in the back room?"

"Sounds right to me," Nicholas said, and he elbowed his way through the faded curtain into the little sitting room behind the shop. We spent a wonderful half-hour there with Mrs. George, helping her sort through a box of hideous jewelry. When the last of the cookies was gone we said good-bye, shouldered our bags, and headed for the bus stop.

"Great place," I said to Nicholas. "I didn't know you father's a doctor. Don't your clothes drive him crazy?"

"Sure," he said. "But my mother dresses funny, too. He says we're the cross he has to bear for being attracted to brains rather than good taste. Blood tells and all that."

When I got home, I showed my new old clothes to Aunt Ellen, but she wasn't especially impressed, although she did her best to act interested.

"You know, Erin, it wouldn't hurt to have some, well, regular clothes, just in case you ever want to dress up," she said.

I pulled out the beautiful pink dress and shawl. "How about this?"

She sighed a very small sigh. "Lovely, dear," she said.

The little guys were crazy about my stuff, though. Cassie and Mimi tried on everything, and Jamie strutted around the house in the jacket for the rest of the day.

"I wish we could . . ." he began, when Uncle Jock heard about my shopping trip.

"Over my dead body," Uncle Jock said. "No offense, Erin, but the truth is that one eccentric is all my blood pressure can handle."

With my spring and summer wardrobe taken care of, I felt ready to tackle nearly anything, including school. But time was not causing Miss Lear to become fonder of me, and the next day in school we had the worst argument yet.

It was over poetry. Miss Lear took ten minutes to

read another of her own compositions to the class. (What possesses some people to read their poetry aloud? Why is it always the people who write such bad stuff that it makes you cringe?)

When she was done, she looked around as if she expected applause. Nicholas burped gently behind his hand and smiled. A girl on the other side of the room began giggling and quit abruptly. I made no attempt to stifle my large, noisy yawn.

"Erin?" Miss Lear said. "Considering your grades in this class, are you certain you feel entitled to that attitude?"

"It's still not Shakespeare," I said. "Since you asked."

"There are some people who find Shakespeare's sonnets maudlin," Miss Lear said, smirking at me.

"What does maudlin mean?" the girl who giggled asked.

"I looked it up once," I volunteered. "It means sentimental. Or poignant. In other words, un-Learlike."

Nicholas shouted with laughter, leaned over and slapped me on the back.

I didn't hurry to the office. After all, going there wasn't a new experience.

After I listened to Mr. Depard for a while, I interrupted and told him I thought he should spend more time worrying about the future of cheating football players and less time worrying about mine, because Miss Lear was hopeless and as long as she was rude to me, I'd be rude to her. Period, end of discussion.

He was still talking about my attitude problem when I strolled out.

I seldom walked with Amelia and her friends between classes, even though we often went in the same direction. I just wasn't into all that giggling and chatter. Sometimes I walked with Val—who also giggled and chattered, but not as much. She seemed to have a need for silence once in a while, too. I never asked her what was bothering her.

Fritzie Seton caught up with me once when I was alone to say, with a sneer, that Val and I seemed to be on pretty friendly terms.

"You feeling left out?" I asked. "If you think I care, think again."

Her sneer disappeared. "I wouldn't be caught dead with Val. She's got the worst reputation in school."

"How odd," I said. "That's what she says about you."

Fritzie never bothered me again. I can't imagine why not.

One day after school, Val asked me to go for a walk with her and have an early dinner at a fast-food place. I called home and asked Aunt Ellen, not telling her that Val was the friend.

"What time will you be home?" Aunt Ellen asked. I could tell by her voice that she was getting ready to fret.

"Oh, early," I said. I'd actually intended going home right after I ate, but Val was shaking her head violently and making all sorts of gestures I didn't understand. "I'll be home before curfew," I told Aunt Ellen.

Val laughed about the curfew. "Why do you put up with it?" she asked as we walked toward the bus stop.

"Who said I put up with anything?" I said. "I don't like hanging around. If I don't have something to do, then I want to go home. Simple."

"Well, I've got plans for us," Val said.

"Like what?"

"You'll see," she said.

53

The fast-food place she took me to was one that was new to me, and I didn't like it much. The food was greasy, and the other people eating there looked sleazy. Before we were halfway through our meal, Val had done enough smiling at two guys to coax them over to our table. They introduced themselves. I didn't bother remembering their names.

The boys asked us if we wanted to go to a party with them when we finished eating. Before I could say anything, Val agreed.

So I disagreed.

"You're kidding!" she exclaimed. "This sounds like fun. Come on. You said yourself you don't go home if you don't want to."

"Who said I didn't want to go home now that I'm through eating?" I stood up, crumpled my napkin, and dropped it on my hamburger. "See you," I said, and I headed for the door.

"Hey, hey!" the guys yelled behind me. "Where are you going? We'll give you a ride."

Sure you will, I thought. The kind of ride my cousin Amelia had, only maybe worse.

I went home, played video games with the little guys for a while, and when Amelia came home from another job with the clown troupe, I helped her give herself a perm.

Val called just before we went to bed. "You missed a great time," she said. "Those guys were really fun."

"Not my type," I said.

"Maybe you'd better reconsider," Val said, sounding angry. "I know you're hoping that Brady Harris is going to take you out, but he won't, you know. He hardly ever dates anybody, and when he does, it's always one of the girls in the orchestra or somebody else like that. It's never, never going to be you."

I nearly asked her why not? But then I remembered that I didn't care. Not a bit. Brady could take out anybody he pleased. I wasn't interested in dating.

But that night while I was lying awake, I wondered what Val thought was wrong with me, besides my clothes and my attitude, I mean.

I wasn't like her! But I wasn't like Amelia, Wendy, and Meg, either.

Suddenly I realized that my fists were clenched so hard that my fingers ached. It took a long time to fall asleep.

I woke up angry, went to school angry, and by the time I reached my history class that afternoon, I was looking for a place to dump my rage.

We had a test, and Bub the no-neck football player had notes written on the inside of his left arm, clear to the elbow.

"If you'd spent the amount of time studying that you spent on cheating, you'd probably pass this test," I said audibly. My voice was shaking with anger.

"You know what happens to finks," Bub hissed.

"No," I said aloud. "Why don't you tell us?"

The history teacher materialized in front of us. "Problems with the test, Erin?" he asked.

"No, only with my seat," I said. "I want to sit somewhere else."

"Wherever you like," the teacher said vaguely. He was concentrating on Bub, who was trying to hide his arm.

I took my test to an empty desk in the front of the room, one that nobody ever sat in. Bub shuffled past me on the way to the door and rammed my head with his elbow as he passed.

"Cute, Bub," somebody said, laughing. Bub slammed the door behind him.

The teacher took his seat, sighing. The clock

ticked. Spring rain pattered on the window, and outside, trees bent in the wind. I wasn't so angry anymore. Getting somebody else in trouble—somebody who deserved it—gave me a mean sense of satisfaction.

When I left class Brady caught up with me in the hall. "I've been trying to talk to you all day," he said. "Would you like to go to a movie Saturday afternoon?"

I almost forgot myself and accepted, but then he added, "Jannie and Mimi are going to the same birthday party. We can drop them off and pick them up after the movie."

Suddenly, without warning, I was ten years old again, standing on a porch and watching the rain come down, waiting and waiting for my family, not knowing yet that I'd never see them again.

I hurried away from Brady without answering. My eyes were on fire.

Chapter 7

Adults crack me up. They want you to learn to take care of yourself and then when you show them that you can, they're angry.

The Castaway

Several days went by without an attack from Miss Lear, and I'd have thought that she'd gotten a tight grip on her nervous condition if she hadn't singled out another girl in class for her spiteful attentions. That girl was more satisfying to Miss Lear than I'd ever been, because she cried.

Just for fun, so that things wouldn't be too quiet for me, I wrote another letter to the newspaper, this time about our school heroes, the football players, who apparently had the idea that school is where you learn how to knock other people around—and who cares whether or not you can read. If you do a good enough job knocking other people around, I wrote, then you get a college scholarship, where you can avoid learning how to read for another four years.

This time my letter didn't show up on the front page, though. Brady printed it in the regular letter column. That was a disappointment, but heck, he was a guy and probably liked football. There's no accounting for what guys like.

"You did it again," Nicholas said, on the afternoon the paper came out. He waved the page with my letter on it in my face.

"What makes you think I wrote that?" I asked.

"Aw, come on, give me a break," he said. "There are only two of us in school, including the teachers, who can see what's wrong with that sports scenario."

I looked him straight in the eye. "Listen, Nicholas, don't you dare tell anybody, or my next letter will be about a short little twerp who's only two months away from going to college and he still has a pacifier hidden away in one of his pockets."

"I do not!" he yelled, bouncing around in rage, with his glasses ready to jiggle right off his nose. "How did you find out about college? I never told anybody."

"You should have read the whole paper, you baby," I said, and I grabbed his copy and turned to the front page, bottom corner, where a tiny, one-inch article said that Nicholas Parrington Brown III had been accepted into the new program at the university—a special one for the highly gifted—and he would start there during summer quarter.

"Who told?" he cried. "Oh, doggone it, somebody told and they promised me it could be a secret, and now what am I going to do?"

"Calm down," I said. "How come you aren't proud of yourself?"

He looked at me in despair. "I am. But I didn't want everybody else to know because they're always teasing me or patting me on the head."

I slung my arm around his shoulder—since we were all alone for a couple of seconds in the hall outside the library. "You'll be famous and everybody will brag about knowing you. And I'll probably never even make it out of high school."

He shrugged off my arm, his face scarlet. "So whose fault is that?"

"I'm no genius," I said.

"Maybe and maybe not," he said. "Mom says that gifted people are sometimes really obnoxious."

"Oh, thanks a lot," I said sourly. "She knows that from her own personal experience with you?"

"She's a psychologist!" he exclaimed. "That's what she does all morning—talk to gifted people who are all screwed up."

"I can't think of anything that would be more fun," I said, "except maybe talking to stupid people who are all screwed up."

"Speaking of Mr. Depard," Nicholas said, with a straight face, "he tried to stop me from entering the program at the U."

"Why?" I asked. "I'd expect him to be glad to get rid of somebody who's smarter than he is and also keeps his shoes tied."

"He said it would make me neurotic."

"So what did you do?"

Nicholas grinned, flashing braces at me. "I told Mom and she called him up and told him—let's see if I can remember how she put it—she said, 'I remember you from high school, Boopie Depard. Stay away from Nicholas or I'll tell everybody how many times you had to take algebra before you finally passed.' "

"Boopie?" I asked. "She called him Boopie?"

"It was his nickname."

"Boopie," I said, sighing happily. "Thanks, Nicholas. You just made me the happiest girl in school."

"Hey, don't tell him where you found out," Nicholas said, and then he added, "Aw, heck, go ahead and tell. In two more months I'm outta here." He nudged me, like a puppy does. "Wish you were coming with me."

"Thanks." I left him there smiling, and I hugged myself. Boopie. Oh, joy. It pays to collect weapons, just in case.

When I got home from school that day, nobody was there. I found a letter for Amelia on the kitchen table—the return address was Fox Crossing. Our cousin Heather wrote to Amelia all the time, and occasionally she even wrote to me. But I never answered. I didn't have anything to say. I didn't write to my grandparents, either, and I was sure they were glad.

I shared a sandwich with the dogs and worked on a sketch for awhile, one that I'd show Mrs. Nugent when it was done. I had drawn Noah's ark with all the animals marching toward it two by two, crowding close and hurrying down a long road that curved back on itself. And here and there, I put in little human figures, urging the animals along. They weren't much more than shadows. But I'd tried to make the animals as perfect as I could. In the background, storm clouds had gathered, and the trees bent in a strong wind.

I turned the sketch upside down to check the proportions, then righted it again. Maybe I'd do it over, this time in watercolors. Would that work better? Or maybe even ink and watercolors. Oh, yes, yes. I began pulling my supplies out of the pantry, where Aunt Ellen had given me a whole cupboard all to myself.

Amelia and her pals came in and caught me. They crowded around my sketch, saying, "That's wonderful!" and "You're really good, Erin. Really!"

I stood there like a stone until they were done talking. Finally I managed to say, "Thanks," and then I gathered up my stuff and went upstairs.

"It's hard to compliment her," I heard Amelia say.

"It's almost as if she'd rather I said something awful."

"She's such a good artist. . . ." Meg or Wendy began. "So good."

I shut the bedroom door and turned on Amelia's stereo.

The next day in school I saw Val walking with a tall, blond boy, one I thought was probably a senior. I'd caught glimpses of him now and then, and chalked him off as one of those useless and boring people who look in mirrors too much. His expensive clothes and his arrogant way of walking told me that he wasn't the sort Val usually hung around with. I was curious, so I walked up and said hello to Val.

She wasn't happy about that. She'd linked her arm with his—and it was easy to see that *he* wasn't happy about *that*. Interesting.

"This is Warren Carey," Val said.

Ah. I remembered the name. The guy who'd attacked Amelia. He was still walking around without crutches? Hmm.

His gaze slid over me and fixed behind me on someone else. He wasn't interested in meeting me.

"This is Erin Whitney, Warren," Val said.

Suddenly Warren was very interested in me. "Whitney?" he asked. "Any relation to Amelia?"

I smiled broadly. "I'm her cousin."

He had the coldest eyes, but I stared him down. He backed up one step, shaking off Val's arm. "See you around, rag bag," he said to me.

"Why not?" I said, grinning. He looked away from me then, and walked away with quick, jerky steps.

"I dated him once," Val said.

"Did you manage to get away?" I asked.

Her mouth tightened. "You heard about Amelia, then. She doesn't know how to play these guys."

I gaped at her. "What do you mean, 'play?'"

"You know," Val said. "Give a little, get a little. Play the game. Guys like to be manipulated."

I was furious! "I don't believe you!" I cried. "He's nothing but a dirty rapist! You know what he wanted from Amelia—and you're talking about giving a little and getting a little. Getting what? Hurt? Dead?"

Val tossed her head and made a face. "That's stupid. He wouldn't have hurt her. He was just trying to see how far he could go. Guys are like that."

"He forced himself on her," I said. I ground my teeth. "You are really dumber than I ever imagined," I told her. "Are you so desperate for a date that you'll let a guy like that use you?"

Her face burned and her eyes filled with tears. "What's wrong with you? Why are you so mad?"

"You're talking about my cousin!" I exclaimed. "You're suggesting that she should have gone along with anything that—that creep!—wanted, just so she could say she went out with him. Well, Mark's a thousand times nicer than Warren. And better looking, too."

"But he's so dull," Val began.

"Did he ever ask you out?" I asked.

"No, but . . ."

"Then you don't know if Mark's dull—and you never will."

I turned my back on her and went to class. Incredible. Where did girls get the idea it was right to be used?

I was in a bad mood, so it was a good thing that the class was art, which always calmed me down. Nicholas, grinning, took out his newest project to show me, and I handed over my watercolor of Noah's ark. It wasn't finished yet—I planned to do it in class—but you could get a good idea of what I was trying to do.

He nodded. "This is wonderful. Perfect." Without asking, he took it up to Mrs. Nugent, and the whole class could hear him say, "Look what Erin brought to school."

Mrs. Nugent held it up for everyone to see, then returned it to me. "When you've finished this, please see me about it," she said. "I have an idea that you might like."

That was the best part of the day.

Val phoned me that afternoon as soon as I got home. Aunt Ellen, busy putting together a meat loaf for dinner, could hear the conversation, and I knew she didn't like Val, so I intended keeping the call short.

"I feel bad about quarreling with you this morning," Val said. "You're my best friend."

Good grief, I thought. We barely knew each other. That was pathetic, *if* she meant it. I remembered that Amelia had said Val didn't like girls—and was manipulative.

"Everything's fine," I said. "What do you want?"

"Don't turn me down until you hear me out," she said. "I'm in the mood for a good movie tonight. Say you'll come with me. We'll have hamburgers first, then see the movie, and you'll be home before nine. Please. Let me make it up to you for what I said about Amelia this morning. I didn't mean it the way you took it, Erin."

It was Friday. There was no reason why I couldn't go, except that Aunt Ellen and Uncle Jock didn't approve of Val. But I was going to be home alone otherwise, because Amelia either worked or went out with Mark on weekends, and my aunt and uncle were taking the little guys to a cartoon festival that night.

63

"What's the movie?" I asked.

Val named one I wanted to see. I chewed my lip, looking at Aunt Ellen, and considering my odds. "Just a minute," I said, and I covered up the mouthpiece.

"I'd like to see this movie," I told Aunt Ellen. "Is it all right with you?"

Aunt Ellen looked grim. "That's Val Guthrie, isn't it?" she said.

I nodded. "But she says I'll be home by nine, even though this is Friday."

"I suppose it's all right," Aunt Ellen said, "if you're really home by nine."

"Okay," I told Val. "Are you driving us?" I knew she'd turned sixteen a few months before and had her driver's license.

"Yes, so I'll pick you up. Thanks, Erin."

I got my jacket and waited on the porch for Val. She picked me up five minutes later, and drove us to a hamburger place north of town, across from one of the smaller shopping malls. She chattered the whole time, mostly about boys, and I was beginning to be sorry I'd agreed to go with her. She also looked peculiar. I don't mean eccentric, I mean cheap, in a too-short leather skirt and mesh panty hose.

Nicholas had told me once that those of us who were eccentric were the worst snobs of all. "We hate the people in regular clothes and also the people who dress like they had more than a passing acquaintance with hired assassins," he told me. "My mother says we are selectively bigoted."

I remember staring at him. "But you said your mother dresses in weird clothes, too, like you."

"That's how come she knows so much about it," he'd told me. Sometimes I wished that I knew her.

The hamburgers were good. We ate quickly,

though, because we planned to see the early movie. We arrived at the theater in plenty of time, and I wanted to find seats, but Val insisted in hanging around the lobby just to check things out, she said. What she meant was that she wanted to check out the guys coming in.

It didn't take long for her to attract the attention of two boys, her usual type, the scary kind. Both of them were interested in her, and I could tell that neither of them wanted to be stuck with me—which was fine, because I had no intention of even learning their names.

"I'm going inside to sit down," I told Val, and I walked off.

Val came running after me with both guys in tow. "Don't do this," she whispered to me, bending over me and practically putting out my eye with a strand of her stiff hair. "They want to go somewhere after the movie."

"So do I," I said. "Home."

"Aw, come on," Val said. "They're fun. We could have a great time."

"They aren't interested in me and I'm not interested in them," I said.

"You could make yourself a little more attractive," she said. "You know, comb out your hair and take off that dumb jacket. I'll let you use my makeup."

I moved over a seat to get away from her. The movie was going to start in a moment, and as far as I was concerned, I was now alone.

"Erin," she whispered. "Please."

"No," I said, loud enough to attract the attention of several people sitting around me. "I'll go home by myself."

I don't know what happened to Val after that—I didn't look around for her. And when the movie was over, I marched straight out of the theater, to the nearest bus stop.

And waited.

And waited some more. At nine-thirty, I figured out that no buses ran on that particular route after eight o'clock. How did I learn that? The sign by the bus stop told me so. Maybe if I hadn't been so angry—at Val and all the rest of the world—I might have noticed it sooner.

So that left me a long way from another bus route. I started walking. Calling home didn't cross my mind.

It was nearly ten-thirty when I finally slipped in the front door. Aunt Ellen and Uncle Jock were watching television, and Uncle Jock shut off the set when I came in.

"Well?" he said.

I explained about the bus.

"Why were you waiting for a bus? I thought Val picked you up." Aunt Ellen looked angrier than I'd ever seen her.

I explained about Val and the boys.

"You should have called us immediately," Uncle Jock said.

"You shouldn't have stayed for the movie," Aunt Ellen said.

"You should have known better than to trust someone like Val," Uncle Jock said.

"Should, shouldn't, should," I said. "Thanks for your understanding. I'm all right—I can take care of myself. I was on brightly lighted streets. I was trying not to be a bother to you. Now that we've got all this straightened out, please excuse me and I'll take a flying leap off the edge of the world. Good night."

They didn't stop me and I didn't go back downstairs for anything that night. When Amelia came home, I was reading in bed.

"I heard about you and Val," she said as she hung up her jacket. "I'm surprised that you didn't see it coming—that she'd want to pick up a couple of guys. She doesn't worry about anything."

"Neither do I," I said. "I handled it."

Amelia looked thoughtful. "I hope you can always handle her. I've seen her do things for no more reason than just stirring up trouble. It's always amazed me that she and Fritzie Seton aren't best friends. Except that Val doesn't seem to have friends."

"She thinks she has me," I said.

"Does she?" Amelia asked.

"Does it matter?" I turned a page in my book.

"You could do a lot better."

"Maybe that's what people tell her about me," I said, not looking up.

Chapter 8

Three kinds of kids walk down the halls by themselves—the loners, the losers, and the lost ones. I don't know which kind I am. Or if it could be fixed.

The Castaway

The letter about the football players, even though it was buried on the editorial page, caused an uproar, to my delight. Unfortunately, somebody on the faculty decided that no more anonymous letters could be printed in the paper. Too bad. The Castaway had other things to say and they wouldn't be heard now.

The end of the Castaway letters didn't make Bub happy, though. He showed up for history every day with a scowl on his thick face. I was tempted to ask him who'd read the letter to him, since it contained more big words than he could manage. But, wisely, I restrained myself. He'd given up grumbling about my being responsible for the teacher catching him cheating—probably because he was going to pass anyway, because football players always pass everything, no matter what—and I didn't particularly want to attract his attention again so soon.

I finished the ark painting, and Mrs. Nugent kept me after class one day to talk about it.

"If you agree, I want to enter this in the state contest," she said. "I'll mat it for you and deliver it myself."

"I won in the grade school division once," I blurted without thinking.

Mrs. Nugent raised her eyebrows. "Well then, they've probably been wondering when they'd see another entry from you."

I couldn't help but grin.

"Winning these contests impresses college scholarship committees," she said. "You're keeping that in mind, I suppose."

"No," I said.

She looked surprised. "Aren't you planning on college? But you must! I know Amelia is."

"I'm not even planning for next week," I told her, and I left before she decided to explore this thought.

I heard more about the contest before the day was over. Brady stopped me outside my history class to tell me that there'd be a notice in the school paper about it. "You're going to enter something, aren't you?" he asked. "I'd love to see you win in the high school division, too."

"I don't know what my plans are yet," I said. Don't ask me why, but I didn't want to tell him what Mrs. Nugent was doing for me.

"But why?" he asked. "Don't you have anything ready? You must—you're always working on something. What does Mrs. Nugent say?"

I sighed. "Come on, Brady," I said. "Give up."

"You'd enjoy winning," he said, with a big grin.

"I don't enjoy anything," I told him, exasperated. "Winning contests is kid stuff."

He linked his arm through mine. "I'm going to keep after you until you agree to submit something. You want to go to the zoo after school? Maybe you'd be inspired there."

I could have told him about the ark painting, but I didn't. Sometimes I caught myself thinking about him in ways that scared me. If I let myself be glad that he seemed to care about me, I could be hurt.

"Hey, it's April," he said. "The zoo's full of baby animals, the sun is shining, and I'll even buy you a hot dog. Say you'll come."

"What about Jannie? Is she coming?" I asked.

"She's going to a children's theater production to-day with the rest of her day-care crowd," he said.

Oh. Now this trip to the zoo was beginning to sound like a date. "I'll have to call Aunt Ellen and tell her where I'm going."

"Fine," he said. "Tell her hello for me."

Sure, I thought. That was no guarantee she'd like the idea.

But she did. So Brady and I went straight to the zoo from school.

The sun was out but the wind was blowing, so I pulled my hat down firmly and buttoned my jacket. We were walking beside the polar bears when Brady said suddenly, "I get a kick out of your clothes."

That surprised me. Brady was, well, pretty ordinary in the clothes department. He dressed like most of the other boys in school, only he was a little neater. Val might be impressed with who he was, but I was sure she would think that he was every bit as dull as Mark.

"Are you going to be part of the clown troupe?" he asked me. "Those kids look like they have a lot of fun."

"I don't want to," I said.

"But you've seen them, haven't you?"

I shook my head. "I hear about it, all the time."

"You really need to see them. Next time they perform, I'll take you. Do you know when it will be?"

70

"They're part of the tenth anniversary celebration for the West Cliff Mall," I said.

"But that's today," he said. "Are they there right now?"

I shrugged. "Maybe. Sometime this afternoon or this evening. I forget what Amelia said."

"You want to go?"

I looked up at him. "I'd honestly rather look at the animals," I told him. "Maybe I'll watch the clowns some other time."

He nodded then, and stopped talking about the clowns. I wasn't sorry.

We found a bench in the sun where we were sheltered from the wind, and ate hot dogs. "I remember eating hotdogs here when I was a little kid," Brady said. "Before Jannie was born. You were living in Seattle then."

"Yes," I said.

"My mother brought me here every week or so. We watched the animals all year round. She had names for them."

I nodded.

He was quiet for a moment, and then he said, "I was so angry when she died."

"You told me," I said. "I'm sorry. Are you over it?"

He shrugged. "I'm not angry anymore. I realized that she didn't want to die. She didn't intend to leave us, to leave Jannie when she's so young."

"No, I don't suppose she did," I said. The conversation was making me uncomfortable. Something deep in my chest hurt. I wanted to get away from the pain, but I didn't want to stand up and walk off. I didn't want to hurt his feelings.

"Sometimes I wonder if you feel that way. Angry

71

because your parents died, I mean. Not able to sort out yet that they didn't do it on purpose.''

I stood up. "I don't want to be rude, Brady, but I never talk about my parents. Never. Now I have to go home.''

He didn't argue. We rode back to my house on the bus, and he came in to talk to my aunt and uncle. They all knew each other, and I might have enjoyed watching him talk to them, except that I kept thinking about what he'd said about his mother. And my parents.

I didn't even want to think about it!

He left finally, after turning down Aunt Ellen's invitation to dinner. "Jannie will be getting back from her field trip pretty soon," he said, "and she'll be looking for me."

After I closed the door behind him, Uncle Jock said, "He has a lot of responsibility for someone his age.''

I went upstairs, not wanting to listen to hymns of praise for Brady "Mr. Perfect" Harris. But even as I started my homework, I thought about his eyes, so serious and kind. And glinting with laughter. He'd found laughter again, I thought, marvelling. The real kind, not the bitter kind.

That evening I got a phone call from Nicholas, which astonished me. But I realized quickly that he didn't consider this a call being made by a boy to a girl. It was just one pal calling another.

"Can you come over to my house?" he asked. "I don't live that far away—or if you want, my mom can come and pick you up."

"What for?" I asked. Did he want someone to play checkers with?

"I was telling Mom about your great clothes, and she wondered if you wanted to see her looms.''

"Her what?" I asked.

"Looms," he said. "You know. Frames for weaving. Mom makes a lot of her clothes from material she weaves herself. She's got stuff lots weirder than yours, and she made it all herself."

I couldn't resist. My aunt and uncle thought it sounded like an interesting visit, and Uncle Jock drove me to the Browns', telling me when we got there that he'd be back in a couple of hours. "School night," he said, as if I didn't remember.

Nicholas bolted out the front door to greet me, followed by several large dogs and a cat with more toes than any I'd ever seen before. "Come in, come in," Nicholas said. "Mom's waiting."

I wasn't sure what to expect when I stepped through the door. Mrs. Brown was even more of a surprise than I could have imagined.

First of all, she didn't look old enough to be anybody's mother, especially somebody Nicholas' age. She didn't look much older than twenty, although that was impossible. Her hair was as long as mine, only pale blond, and it hung loose and straight to her waist. She wore a woven headband with flowers worked into the fabric. It matched her ankle-length skirt.

"That's the most beautiful skirt I ever saw," I said, even before Nicholas introduced us.

"From what Nick told me about you, I thought you might like it." She held it out at the sides, so I could see. "Come with me. I'll show you my looms. Nick says you're an artist. Well, there's a lot an artist can do with fabrics, and I wanted you to see."

She led me into a long room with a bare floor. Several looms were set up, wide ones and narrow ones, and on each I saw beautiful fabric—stripes and patterns and florals.

"I thought you were a psychologist," I blurted.

73

"I am," Mrs. Brown said, "but that doesn't mean I don't have an imagination. Everybody ought to be able to do more than one thing. Otherwise, life can get pretty dull."

Nicholas hung around listening while she explained to me how the looms worked, and how she designed her patterns. She showed me lengths of fabric she'd made before, and other material that she'd embroidered. The room was full of magic. And Mrs. Brown was magical, from her hair to her flowing skirt to the bracelets she wore. Bracelets of colored stone set in silver.

She saw me looking at them. "Yes, I made these, too. Here, take one." She pulled off a bracelet set with pale pink and blue stones and slipped it over my hand.

"I don't think I should," I said.

"Of course you should. And I have a skirt length for you, too." She pulled open a drawer and lifted out folded material. "Nick told me you like unique things and animals, and he remembered that I'd made this a couple of years ago. You seem like the perfect person to have it. I got my ideas at the zoo." And then she laughed.

I unfolded the material and saw, woven into the pale rose background, every animal I'd seen that afternoon—the elephants and tigers and camels—even the meerkats. They peered from behind leaves and around the trunks of trees and between blades of grass. I'd never seen anything like it.

"It's too beautiful for a skirt," I said. "It ought to be on a wall."

"If you put it on a wall, I'll take it back," she said. "It's meant to be worn—and who cares what anybody thinks, right?"

Suddenly the three of us were laughing like idiots.

"Who cares?" Nicholas cried, and he threw up his

arms and did a silly little dance. "Nobody but Boopie Depard!"

And the three of us laughed even harder.

When I got home, I showed Aunt Ellen the bracelet and the skirt length. She said what I had—the fabric ought to be on a wall.

"But Mrs. Brown said she'd take it back if I didn't make it into a skirt. Only I don't know how to sew."

"Then I'll teach you," Aunt Ellen said. She held the fabric up. "No one else will have anything like this." She looked at me, then, and her smile faded.

"Of course," she said quietly. "I'm sorry it took Mrs. Brown to recognize what you needed. I should have seen it myself."

"What do you mean?" I asked.

"You only wanted to be different from the crowd, didn't you?" she asked. "The clothes, I mean. You only wanted to be different from the rest of them, and your grandparents—and us, too—we all thought you were rebelling against something. We just didn't know what."

I folded up my skirt length and mumbled something—I can't remember what. As quickly as possible, I escaped upstairs.

Rebelling? Or wanting to be different?

Or just refusing to accept anything about this stupid world, no, not anything—not the clothes or the behavior or the school or the kids. That wasn't rebelling or wanting to be different. That was wanting not to exist anymore.

I looked out the bedroom window at the dogs playing in the backyard. Not my dogs. Not my backyard. Not my house.

Not my family.

I sat down on the bed and held the material to my chest and cried.

Chapter 9

I had my own cat once but he died. Now I prefer
to draw pictures of imaginary cats. They never
lived, so nothing can happen to them.

The Castaway

Another football player was caught cheating at
school, and you'd have thought that the end of the
world was only minutes away. The kids were divided
about evenly over whether or not the guy should be
suspended. Bub hadn't been, but some people—me
included—figured that nothing short of suspension
would be fair.

Not that suspension cured anything. I ought to
know.

Bub got mad all over again, and directed his anger
at me in our history class.

"You started this," he grumbled at me one afternoon.

"Started what?" I asked as I pulled out my sketch
pad.

"This big flap over taking tests. My dad says that
tests aren't the way to find out whether or not a guy
knows what's been happening in class."

"How does your dad propose to measure how much
you've learned in here, then?" I asked as my pencil
flew.

"Huh?" he grunted. "Why do you always talk like

that, as if you know everything and everybody else is stupid?''

"I usually don't," I said. "I only talk like that when I'm in the presence of a superior intellect."

"You been hanging around with that Nicholas kid," Bub said. "He thinks he's so funny, talking like I didn't understand him."

"Nicholas is only fourteen," I said. "You have to make allowances for his lack of respect." I ripped the page out of my sketch book and handed it to him. "Here. Keep this to remember me by when you're rich and famous."

"Why would I want to remember you?'' he asked. He wasn't being sarcastic. He genuinely wanted to know.

"Don't worry about it," I said, patting his hand. "You just be happy instead."

He grunted again and looked down at the sketch. "What is this?''

"It's your head," I said. I'd drawn circles, one inside the other, on and on until the smallest was not much bigger than a dot. "See? This outer layer is your hair and this next layer is your skin. Then comes bone. It's pretty thick. Next is muscle and then fat. Here's a layer of plain air. This little circle in the middle is your brain. Don't tip your head over too far to one side because it will fall out your ear."

He stared at the drawing for a long time, then slowly crumpled it into a ball. "I wasn't going to ask you for a date anyway," he said, which was probably his idea of the worst insult he could deliver.

I clutched my chest. "Oh, be brave, my heart," I said.

I was still laughing to myself when I got home that afternoon. Aunt Ellen was waiting for me, and I couldn't read her expression. "I need to talk to you," she said.

"Sure. Where are the little guys?"

"Playing across the street," she said. "I wanted some time alone with you."

Great, I thought. Now what have I done? I sat down at the kitchen table with her and accepted the cup of hot chocolate she pushed toward me.

"It's about your clothes," she said. "Yours. And now Mimi's and Cassie's. They admire you very much. They want clothes like yours, and when I refused to take them to a thrift shop, they did the best they could with old play clothes and their brother's cast-offs. I fight this battle every morning."

I hadn't noticed. The girls looked fine to me and I told Aunt Ellen so.

"Yes," she said with a big sigh. "They do because I send them back to change until they get it right. I can't tell you how to dress, Erin. You're too old. I've given up hoping you'd want clothes like Amelia's—I understand that I don't have a right to inflict my taste on you. I've even hoped that Mrs. Brown would be an influence on you—weaving odd, artistic clothes is fine. Different but still fine. Wearing cast-off rags simply isn't."

"They're clean," I said. "What more do you want?"

She reached over and plucked open my prison farm sweater. Underneath, I wore a peach satin blouse and green velvet vest embroidered in gold thread. My skirt was long and black, my favorite because of the huge pockets. "I don't know what I want," she said, and she sounded exhausted. "I only know that your clothes are so tacky that I could cry when you go out of here in the morning."

"Worried about the neighbors?" I asked. "Grandmother was always worried about hers."

Aunt Ellen shook her head, then nodded it, then shook it again. "I don't know. I hate myself for this conversation, but you are influencing Mimi and Cassie. Right now they think it's all just fun. But you know as well as I do that pretty soon when they're older it won't be fun anymore, and they'll be hurt by the other children because they're too different. And it's not a difference they chose after long consideration of all the options—they're only babies. It's a difference they chose because they love you so much."

"Sorry," I said, and I really meant it. "I don't want to hurt them. I'll tell them that they should do what you say."

Uncle Jock had come in and was leaning against the door, listening. I glanced over at him and said, "Sorry, Uncle Jock."

He heaved a giant sigh. "I think we should all leave each other alone," he said. "Clothes are clothes. I've been giving this some thought, and the more I see of Erin around here, the more I think we should dress the way we please. I've had some of my biggest laughs lately watching Erin go out of here in some new, outlandish outfit. Laughs aren't always easy to come by in this world."

"But you're still wearing suits to your office," I said.

He grinned. "Don't do as I do, do as I say," he said.

Nothing was solved by the conversation, since Aunt Ellen still felt that Mimi and Cassie should wear their regular school clothes. But I was now aware in the mornings of the bickering that was going on down the hall while my little cousins were dressing. One morning I intruded, knocking quickly and then opening the

79

door just as Aunt Ellen was pulling one of Jamie's old sweatshirts off Cassie.

I scowled at the little guys. "Put on your school clothes and quit acting like such jerks."

"But you . . ." began Cassie.

"I'm a jerk," I said, and I shut the door behind me when I walked out.

Amelia was waiting in the hall, grinning. "Thanks," she said. "Mom was beginning to worry a lot about that situation."

"What chance do the girls have?" I said. "I dress like a bag lady every day and you do it when you're working. Together we can ruin the world."

We walked to school together that morning—something I tried to avoid most of the time—and, even though I refused to discuss my own choice of clothes, I promised Amelia that I'd continue to discourage her little sisters from copying me.

"Are you going to make a skirt out of the material Mrs. Brown gave you?" Amelia asked me.

"I would if I knew how to sew. Do you?"

"Yes, but I don't have much time these days. Mom would show you, and she'd love doing it. She's really good. I'll bet you would be, too." Amelia wasn't looking at me, but I was conscious of how hard she was trying to persuade me to change my ways. Who would actually sew bag lady clothes? If she got me sewing, maybe I'd end up dressing better.

"I'll think about it," I said. But not much or very often, I added to myself. I really didn't want to spend time brooding about why I dressed the way I did. There was something painful down the end of that road. I didn't want to poke it with a stick and see how bad it could hurt me. Maybe I was hiding inside my rags. Maybe I had plenty to hide from.

Brady asked me to come to dinner at his house the

next day. I was going to turn him down, but I remembered Jannie and my promise of a drawing lesson, so I agreed to go. We went to the park after school and fed the squirrels the sandwich I hadn't eaten at lunch. At five, we walked to the day-care center and picked up Jannie, then walked to the Harris house.

Mr. Harris, in an apron, was in the kitchen frying chicken. After we'd been introduced, he said, "I hope you like chicken and baked beans. They're Jannie's favorites, and she was sure they'd be yours."

They weren't, but Jannie was watching my face, so I smiled and said there was nothing I liked better. "You want a drawing lesson while we're waiting for dinner?" I asked her.

"Yes, but first, come and see our kitties." She dragged me by the hand into the playroom in the basement and showed me a mother cat, a beautiful Persian, and her four babies.

I knelt beside the box and Jannie put one of the kittens in my cupped hands. "We could draw this one," she said. "This is Alexander. He's going to be my very own cat, forever."

Alexander's eyes weren't open yet, and I suspected that his mother would like me better if I weren't holding her baby, so I tucked him back beside her and told Jannie that we'd draw the whole box full. "But first we'll start with the box," I said. I took out my sketch book and started her out.

Many pages later, she finally had a box that looked something like a box. "Now we fill it with cats," I said, and I showed her about drawing shapes first, ovals and circles and oblongs for the different body parts. "See how easy it is?"

She was intent on her work and didn't answer, but Brady was watching and smiling. "Dad hates to interrupt, but dinner's on the table," he said.

"Just a minute," Jannie said.

I took the paper away and said, "It'll wait. Honestly. That's one nice thing about drawing. It waits for you for as long as you need."

The four of us sat in the kitchen, my favorite place in any house, and we had a wonderful time. Mr. Harris didn't stare at my clothes or make comments, but instead told us one funny story after another about his boyhood on a farm in Montana. I liked him, and I thought that he liked me.

When it was time for me to leave, Mr. Harris said, "I've already cleared this with your aunt and uncle, Erin. If you want one of Shasta's kittens when they're old enough to leave her, we'd be glad to see you take one. Any except Alexander, of course, because he's already spoken for."

For a moment, I was tempted. The kittens were beautiful, and I'd have loved a pet of my own. But life takes more away than it ever gives, so I shook my head. "Thanks," I said. "But it's better if I don't."

Mr. Harris seemed surprised, but he didn't argue. Only Jannie kept saying, "Are you sure? Don't you want one? Are you really and truly sure?"

On the way home, Brady asked me if I wanted time to think about it. "You don't have to decide today," he said. "They're only a week old."

I shook my head firmly. "I can't, but it was really nice of you and your dad to offer."

"But why can't you?" he said, mystified.

"Because because because!" I shouted. "Let it alone, Brady, okay?"

"Okay," he said. "Subject closed."

I lay awake a long time that night, not thinking about anything except the dark. The long, cold, empty dark.

The next day at school during lunch break, I saw

Warren Guthrie walking with Fritzie Seton. She knew about Amelia and still she let that monster walk close enough to her to touch. I couldn't believe it. I was already mad at the world, and that sight only made me feel worse.

I must have been staring, because he stopped in front of me and narrowed his eyes.

"Get lost, Erin," Fritzie said.

"No, *you* get lost," Warren said to her. He didn't take his eyes off me.

Fritzie, her face scarlet, sucked in her breath and hurried away. I was so startled that my guard dropped, and when Warren moved toward me, herding me against the wall, I couldn't think straight.

He leaned his arms against the wall, one on each side of me. "I'd like to know you better," he said.

I recovered from my surprise, scowled, and stuck my hands in my pockets the way the tough kids do. "Buzz off," I said.

Grinning, he touched my side, poking with one finger. "Whatcha got under those rags?"

"This!" I cried, and I pulled my fist out of my pocket and hit him straight on his nose.

"Ow!" he yelled.

"Are we done talking yet?" I asked, "because I'm busy."

He was gasping and dancing around, holding his hands over his bleeding nose. "You . . . you . . . you . . ." he shouted. "Why did you do that?"

"Because it was fun, you toad," I said. And I walked off laughing.

That was for you, Amelia, I thought.

Chapter 10

What is there to talk about when there's no one left who remembers what Christmas was like at your house when you were a little kid?

The Castaway

I was suspended for two weeks for punching Warren Carey. If I'd been a boy who'd given a girl a bloody nose, I bet Boopie Depard would only have suspended me for a week.

We had an interesting meeting in the principal's office the day after I committed my mind-boggling crime. Warren's parents were there, along with my aunt and uncle and Mr. Depard. And poor, suffering Warren, of course.

I listened while the principal and the Careys told me how rotten I was to have deliberately bloodied his nose. When they were done, I said, "If he ever tries to feel my chest again, I'll *break* his stupid nose."

When the yelling stopped, I told them I'd changed my mind. My aunt and uncle looked bewildered. The Careys looked triumphant.

"If he touches me again," I told Mr. Carey, "I'll come by your house and break *your* nose." I pulled my hat down and smiled. "Believe me," I added. "And Warren's a seventeen-year-old dirty old man, as if you didn't already know. You should also know that I don't forgive anybody. I get even."

The Careys said I needed a psychiatrist.

"You think I need a shrink because I don't want a pervert feeling me up in the main hall at school?" I asked. "Somebody's crazy, but it's not me."

The Careys said somebody ought to call the police.

"Yes, yes," I cried and I grabbed for the phone on the principal's desk. "I'll do it, and I'll tell them what he did to Amelia, too. That's a story that'll interest them."

The Careys left, taking Warren with them. My aunt and uncle told the principal and Mr. Depard that they didn't want to hear another word about Warren Carey, ever. And then we Whitneys marched out.

"Next time," my uncle said to me when we were home again, "if there is a next time, would you mind socking him when there are no witnesses? I hate paying Warren's bills."

"I'm sorry you have to pay his doctor," I told Uncle Jock. "But that's all I'm sorry about."

"Me, too," Uncle Jock said. "Let's all go out to dinner and celebrate. Not Warren's nose, mind you. But that you successfully defended yourself."

"I'd just as soon celebrate his nose, too, if you don't mind," Aunt Ellen said. "I've always wished Amelia had broken something on him. Aren't we awful?"

"Yes," I said. "See how much fun it can be?"

According to Nicholas, I became instantly famous at school. He came by and told me that even Bub was impressed.

"He asked me if you'd studied Karate," Nicholas said. "But I told him that you were just naturally mean."

During my two weeks at home, I spent most of my days helping Aunt Ellen in her garden. The weather was wonderful, Aunt Ellen didn't talk much, and I

85

began feeling peaceful for the first time in ages. But then this changed quickly.

Amelia told me one afternoon that our cousin Heather was coming for a visit. "I thought she'd like going to the spring dance with me—she'll get to see all her old friends in one place."

"Doesn't she have a boyfriend in Fox Crossing?" I asked. "Won't he mind if she goes to a dance with somebody else?"

"Oh, she won't have a date. She'll just go along with Mark and me. And we thought you might like to do that, too. Not everybody has a date."

"I don't want to go to a dance," I said.

"But Heather would love it if you came, too," Amelia pleaded. "She's bringing a long dress. . . ."

"Why?" I asked. "What kind of dance is this?"

Amelia laughed. "I thought you read the school paper. And there are posters up all over the school. It's formal. It's the one formal dance all year, except for the senior prom. Come on, say you will. Mom's taking me shopping next weekend. We'll find something great for you, too, and you'll have a wonderful time."

I scowled. "I don't want a long dress and I don't want to go to the dance. I hate that sort of thing. Why can't you just let me alone?"

Amelia bit her lip and walked out of the room.

The next afternoon while Aunt Ellen was grocery shopping, Val came by. School wasn't out yet, but little things like that never bothered Val. "How are you doing?" she asked. "You've been away from school for so long that everybody's starting to forget about you."

"Suits me," I said. We sat in the kitchen, sharing a soft drink. I didn't particularly want her to stay, but I wasn't anxious for her to leave, either. Sometimes I got sick of my own company.

"Are you going to the dance?" she asked.

"Of course not," I said. "I don't like dances, and who would I go with?" I didn't tell her about Amelia's invitation. I had a hunch Val wouldn't relate too well to going dancing without a date.

"What about Brady?" she asked. "He'd probably take you." She studied me thoughtfully for a moment. "If you did something about your clothes."

"I'm not doing anything about my clothes," I said. "You sound like Amelia and her friends."

"Oh, well, Amelia," she said, and I was sure she wanted to add that what could you expect from Amelia but impossible demands and ridiculous notions. Not that she hadn't just made a comment herself about my clothes. "I suppose she's going with Mark."

"And Heather. Heather's coming from Fox Crossing for the weekend, so she can go to the dance and see all her old friends."

"Great fun," Val said crossly. "Miss Ideal Sophomore and her double. Well, I'm going to the dance, but I don't know who's taking me yet. Mike said that he would, if he didn't have to dress up too much, and Stan said he would if we could leave early, because he's been invited to a party in West Seattle and he wants to check that out, too."

I didn't care if she went with somebody's pet pig, but I kept quiet. The whole business of the dance was irritating me.

Amelia came home before Val had left, and they barely spoke. After Val had gone home, Amelia told me again that Val was bad news. "Nothing is ever simple with her," she said. "She's a troublemaker. That Mike she's been going around with—he'd already asked a girl to the dance, but Val went to work on him and the next thing, he'd broken the date. Now she's been telling people that maybe she'll go with somebody else."

"They aren't your friends," I said. "What do you care?"

Amelia looked embarrassed. "You're right. It isn't any of my business. But I wish you'd keep away from her and the guys she knows. Sooner or later you'll get involved and wish you hadn't."

I shrugged and picked up the book I'd been reading earlier in the day. "I can't see Val as being all that popular with boys," I said.

"She isn't," Amelia said. "But she manipulates everybody. Boys end up going out with her even when they don't want to."

I turned a page and said, "Hmm. Maybe she's lonely. I don't really care."

Amelia wandered off and I drew a deep breath. I didn't need her advice about anything. You'd think she'd be grateful for what I'd done to Warren and stop trying to drag me into things like that dance. She thought Val was manipulative? She did a pretty good job herself.

I could hear her on the phone, babbling to Wendy about the clowns and some party they were performing at the next afternoon, and I decided I had to get out of there. I grabbed my jacket and headed for the park. I sat for a while watching squirrels, then I walked past Brady's house. Should I see if he was home? Would he take my showing up the wrong way? I only wanted to see the kittens—and a chance to talk to somebody who wasn't trying to reform me.

I finally got up enough courage to ring the doorbell. He came, surprised to see me. "Did you change your mind about the kitten?" he asked.

"No, but I'd like to look at them again."

He led me downstairs and I sat by the box for a while, watching the mother give her children a good washing. "They're so cute," I said.

Brady was quiet for a moment, then he said, "I've missed you around school."

"Does Warren?" I asked, and laughed.

He laughed, too. "He hasn't been there. Somebody said his family had sent him back to California to rest up."

"From me?"

Brady shrugged. "I think maybe things were catching up with him."

"Would you like to walk in the park for a while?" I asked suddenly. I didn't want to talk about Warren anymore. "There are half a dozen squirrels hanging around the pond. At least there were a few minutes ago."

"I'll bring some bread for them," he said, and we hurried up the stairs.

The squirrels were still there, as if they were waiting for us. We sat side by side on a bench and tore up bread for them. One, too impatient to wait his turn, jumped up on the bench beside me, close enough to touch.

"They get spoiled," Brady said.

Some children ran by, trailing balloons behind them. They'd obviously just come from a party.

I swallowed hard. Had I ever been that young?

"Jannie has such a good time at parties," Brady said. "I wish I could find one for her to go to every day. She still misses our mother. So do I. I wonder if there'll ever come a time when I don't half expect to find her there when I get home from school."

With a sharp pang, I remembered the artist on the waterfront stairs who looked for his dead wife in crowds. I told Brady about him, and Brady nodded slowly. "Yeah," he said. "I do that, too."

We watched the squirrels climb the nearest tree. A dog was coming. The squirrel chattered angrily.

"Did you get to tell your mother good-bye?" I asked.

"No, not exactly," Brady said. "She was in the hospital, and she kept telling me not to worry, that she'd be home soon. But I could see her getting thinner and . . . One day my dad came to school. I knew as soon as I saw him that she had died." He reached down for a pebble and tossed it into the pond. "I don't think I could have said good-bye. Maybe she knew that."

I couldn't look at him anymore. "I would have liked to say good-bye to my parents. They were killed while I was at a birthday party. They took me there, but I didn't say good-bye. I just jumped out of the car and ran for the porch. I didn't look back. The last time I saw them was over the back of the car seat. They were smiling. I wish I'd said good-bye." I shoved my hands in my pockets, hard. "My mother was wearing a blue shirt, and her hair was in a ponytail. My dad had cut himself shaving, and you could see the place on his chin. . . ."

I stood up abruptly. "I'm going home," I said.

Brady walked along beside me, but he didn't talk. When we got to my house, he said, "I have to run now to get Jannie. Would you like to go to the Market tomorrow afternoon? We could look for your friend."

I shrugged and said, "Sure." I headed inside, and when I looked back, he was already running toward the end of the block.

When I got up to the room I shared with Amelia, she was prancing around in her Tiny Tina costume, but she was wearing a different wig. "Do you like this one better?" she asked me. "Tell me what you honestly think."

"It looks fine," I said.

I went into the bathroom and held my face in a

90

towel until I was sure I wasn't going to cry. Poor Brady. He hadn't wanted to say good-bye, but he could have. He knew it was coming. Did that make it worse? The knowing?

Chapter 11

Some days are a big pain. Everybody I know acts as if he has his thumb in his mouth and his mind in neutral.

                                        The Castaway

Brady and I went to the waterfront. The wind was blowing hard and smelled of salt water and, I thought, far-off places I'd never see. We rode the old trolley, then bought french fries to throw to the sea gulls. When it seemed that rain would fall any moment, we climbed the stairs to the market.

I looked for the artist, but he wasn't there, and I was more disappointed than I imagined I could be over a stranger. Or maybe he wasn't a stranger. The artist and I had something in common—we looked for people we'd never see. I wanted Brady to meet him. We'd have been a company of three then. Crowd-searchers.

Brady and I leaned on the stair railings and looked out at the water.

"Did you ever come here with your parents?" he asked.

I'd forgotten. Suddenly a memory came crashing back, and for a moment I was in such pain that I nearly groaned. Yes, my parents had brought me here. My dad bought a whole salmon at the market, and my mother bought cut flowers and bead jewelry and a watercolor of a quail.

"Did they?" Brady asked again, almost absent-mindedly. He was watching sea gulls.

"No," I lied. "Let's go home. It's going to rain any second."

"Sure," Brady said. We started up the rest of the stairs. "What's wrong?"

"Nothing."

"Did I say something I shouldn't have?"

"No. Everything's fine," I said.

"You're acting as if you're angry with me."

"I'm not!" I cried. "But I'm going to be if you don't shut up!"

He didn't say anything until we reached our bus stop. Rain was coming down hard, and we stood in a doorway to keep dry.

"Erin, you're upset because I asked you about your parents," he said.

I turned my head away and looked down the street. *Where was the bus?*

"I'm sorry," he said. "Yesterday, you seemed to want to talk, and I thought . . ."

"I don't want to talk about them," I said. "I'm sorry I told you anything."

"Sometimes it helps to talk about things," he began, but I interrupted him.

"Some people whine about everything all the time," I said. "They yap for a week about a broken fingernail. They have an argument with somebody and then tell you about it a hundred times a day until you'd do anything to shut them up."

Brady looked down at me and then away. "This is different," he said.

"No, it isn't. What's done is done. There's no point

in talking about it, because you can't change anything.''

"Sometimes people need a chance to talk about things until they don't hurt so much anymore," Brady said, his voice quiet and patient.

"Leave me alone!" I shouted. "What's wrong with you, anyway? Why can't you just shut up about it?''

I didn't wait for him to answer, but instead ran away from him, heading up hill. I didn't look back, but I didn't hear him following me. After a while I stopped at another bus stop. The rain let up, and by the time a bus came, it had stopped falling and a pale sun broke through the clouds.

I went to the university district and walked through the campus until I reached the building where my father had taught art. I looked up at it for a long time, not remembering the past but thinking about the future. Would I be a student here? Would I sit in the classroom where he'd looked out the windows at the sky and maybe thought of me?

At home, dinner was over by the time I got there, but my aunt hadn't been expecting me since she'd known I was going to the waterfront. I was hungry, though, and explained that I hadn't eaten because I'd been so busy. Nobody asked what I'd been so busy doing, thank goodness. I didn't want to explain anything else for the rest of my life.

Heather phoned Amelia that evening, and they talked for a long time. From Amelia's side of the conversation, I gathered that Heather was looking forward to seeing me again. I didn't hear Amelia say that I wasn't going to the dance with them. I had a hunch she was keeping her fingers crossed that I'd change my mind.

Later, Brady called me. Amelia answered the phone, and when she told me who was calling, I told her to say that I'd gone to bed. She argued for a moment, but I settled things by going up to our bedroom and slamming the door. I didn't know what she finally told him and I didn't care. Life goes on. And on and on.

When I went back to school, Miss Lear smirked at me and said, loud enough for everyone to hear, that I probably wouldn't be passing the course because of all the days I'd missed.

I simply looked at her. What was I supposed to say?

But a quick thought flickered through my mind. If I kept this up, I wouldn't be sitting in my father's old classroom. The university wouldn't want me.

Mrs. Nugent kept me after art class for a moment to tell me that the time had come to officially enter my painting of the ark in the state contest. My first impulse was to refuse, but Nicholas, who was shamelessly eavesdropping and jittering around like a monkey, said, "You've gotta do it, Erin. You've gotta do it."

I shrugged and agreed finally. But I wasn't going to tell my aunt and uncle or Amelia—or anyone. I swore Nicholas to secrecy, threatening him with the direst punishment if he blabbed.

"You going to punch me out like you did Warren?" he asked, delighted with the conversation. "I told my mom about that."

"What did she say?"

"She said she'd have done the same thing. You're famous, you know. Some of us wanted to put your name on a plaque in the hall."

"I'll bet Mr. Depard thought that was a great idea," I grumbled.

"Actually, no," Nicholas said.

95

"You talked to him about it?" I asked incredulously.

"Sure. I even designed a sort of coat of arms, with a fist punching a nose. I thought it was quite good, but when I showed it to him, he said I was pressing my luck." Nicholas didn't seem to mind pressing his luck.

"Well, no matter what happens, you're out of here pretty soon," I said.

"Mom says there's a special summer program for young artists at the university," he said. "She's going to get the information and give it to your aunt. And you know Mrs. Nugent would put in a good word for you. I'll be in summer school there—we could have a great time."

I looked down at the little twerp and laughed. "I can see you now, big man on campus. The squirrels will carry you off to keep with the rest of their nuts."

Even though I laughed, I was pleased at the thought of a summer art program. Might it be possible for me?

Not unless I managed somehow to salvage my reputation at school. Even thinking about that gave me a headache. Nothing was worth whatever it would take to make peace with Miss Lear and Mr. Depard.

Several times during the day I ran into Brady, but I kept away from him, even turning my back when he tried to talk to me. Being around him made me feel like I was on my way to the dentist. Pain was coming, and I didn't want any part of it.

That afternoon when I got home, I found that Aunt Ellen had dragged a folding cot down from the attic and put in the bedroom I shared with Amelia. There was barely room for it—and I wondered who was going to be sleeping in it. Me? Wasn't I the unwanted intruder?

Aunt Ellen, tucking sheets in firmly, said, "Heather won't mind this for a couple of nights. I thought about putting one of the little guys in it, but you know how they are. The cot would end up folded, with them in it, and the whole household in an uproar again."

"Maybe I should take it," I said. Might as well get it over with.

"Of course not," Aunt Ellen said briskly. "The cot's comfortable enough for a short visit. Next August, if Heather comes for the whole month the way she usually does, we'll get something better. Maybe a trundle bed."

I thought to myself that when August came, they might be sick of me, and then Heather could have my bed because I'd be long gone. Aunt Ellen and Uncle Jock had so far managed to keep from going into a decline over me the way my grandparents had, but I knew I was one of those people who don't wear well—like shoes that are too tight. I didn't know how to fix that, and I wasn't sure I even wanted to try.

Brady called me again. Uncle Jock answered that time, and I still refused to accept the call. Later Val called me, just to chat, she said, but before the conversation was over she'd asked me a dozen questions about Heather coming.

I got the vague feeling that she was jealous of my cousins, but I didn't understand why. They led such conventional lives—she could do the same if she wanted. Nobody was making her wear green mascara and four earrings in one ear. There weren't many girls in school who dressed and acted like Val, but there were some, so she had her own kind to pal around with. I had no idea why she wanted to hang around with me instead, especially since I was in to thrift shop clothes, art, books, and walks in the park instead of picking up guys.

Answering one of Val's questions, I said, "I don't know what Heather's long dress is like. Why are you asking?"

Val laughed. "I wanted to be sure I'd be wearing the uniform of the day."

"Ha," I said. "I'll bet the dress you wear won't look anything like what either of my cousins has. Quit kidding me."

"You're going to change your mind about going, you know," Val predicted. "I know you will. You'll figure out how much fun we'd have, and get yourself something gorgeous. I'm willing to bet on it."

"You'll lose," I said. "I hate those long party dresses, your kind and Amelia's kind both. And I hate dances."

"Amelia and Heather are probably glad you're not going," Val said.

"What?" I asked, startled. "Why should they be?"

There was a moment of silence. "Oh, I don't know," Val said. "Forget I said anything."

"No, I want to know what you mean," I said.

"Gotta go," she said. "Somebody's at the door and I'm the only one home." And she hung up. She *was* jealous of my cousins!

But I sat there for a long time, thinking about what she'd said. What if Amelia really didn't want me to go? Well, it didn't matter. I wasn't going and so that was that. And I didn't care what she thought of me, she or Heather.

But who were they to hope I *wouldn't* go!

They were really close—I knew that. Almost like sisters. They supported each other, no matter what. And they had everything—parents, other kids in the house. Sure, they had problems sometimes—Amelia had to deal with Warren and all the trouble he caused her. And Heather, according to Amelia, went through a lot after she moved to Fox Crossing, with a house-keeper who tried to hurt her dog and some rotten kids at school who'd tried to cheat her stepsister out of a scholarship. But still, they didn't know what real trouble was.

They didn't know what it was like to have a family album full of pictures of people who didn't exist anymore.

They didn't know how lucky they were. And I was jealous, too. But who cared about that, either?

I sat on the floor and hugged the dogs.

Chapter 12

Some people are like a blister on your heel. The
only thing you learn from them is that you
shouldn't have tried so hard.

The Castaway

I hated myself when I thought nasty things about
my cousins. So I set about trying to make myself
more agreeable all around. I smiled at Amelia whenever I saw her. I even made her bed in the morning
as well as my own—Amelia was so busy those days
that she didn't have time for much of anything except
her school work and her clown troupe. I even went
to see the clowns in action the next day after school,
when they were performing at a street fair a few
blocks away.

But I couldn't seem to get the hang of being a
proper cousin. I learned that on the afternoon when I
asked the little guys if they'd like to go to the park
with me to feed the squirrels.

"We can't," Cassie said. "We're making plans to
paint a sign for Heather."

"A big sign," Mimi explained, gesturing with her
arms. "It's going to say, Welcome Home Heather."

"But she lives in Fox Crossing now," I said.

Mimi stared at me as if I'd lost my mind. "This is
always going to be her real and true home. Always
and forever."

I got the hint and went to the park by myself. There were a lot of little kids there that afternoon, so many that they had to wait in line for the swings. I watched them, every one a stranger to me, but I didn't draw them. There were birds in the park, too, and the squirrels, of course. And a pair of ducks solemnly paddling in the small lily pond. I sat down at the water's edge and drew them.

To my surprise, Val showed up and stood beside me, looking down at my sketch. "Cute," she said.

"How'd you know I was here?"

"Your aunt told me. I didn't have anything else to do so I decided to walk over and check the place out." She looked around at all the little kids. "I didn't even waste my time here when I was their age. I sure wouldn't do it now. You want to go somewhere for something to eat?"

I shook my head. "I want to finish this."

She sat down gingerly on the grass, trying to manage her short skirt and high heels, sighing to let me know she was sacrificing a lot for me. "How long are you going to be?"

"As long as it takes," I said. "How come you were looking for me?"

"I had an idea that I thought you might like hearing about." She fidgeted around and finally stood up again. "I hate this. Can't we go for a walk or something? I feel like any minute one of those ducks is going to bite me—or maybe one of those bratty little kids will."

I shoved my sketch book in one of my big pockets and got to my feet. "Okay. Let's go across the street and have a soft drink. Then you can tell me what's on your mind. Is that okay?"

"Sure." She minced along beside me, her heels

clacking on the sidewalk. "I've just about given up on getting you a date with a guy," she said.

"Good," I told her. "That's the smartest thing you've said yet."

"Of course, you've got Brady," she said. "Or you hope you do."

"I don't have Brady or anybody else," I told her. "Is that what this conversation is all about?"

We'd reached the sandwich shop and found a table near the window, then ordered. Val checked her makeup before she tasted her soft drink and again afterward. I had to wait forever before she answered me.

"I know I cut you off the other day when you wanted to know what I meant about Amelia and Heather not really wanting you to go to the dance," she said finally.

"So?"

"Well, they don't," she said. "Think about it. Why would Amelia want to go with you when everybody in school calls you Weird Whitney or Bag Lady right in front of her? I've heard them do it."

"Thanks," I said bitterly. "I needed to hear that."

She arched her plucked eyebrows. "What did you expect? It's what you wanted, isn't it? I mean, why else would you dress the way you do?"

I nodded. She had a point. But I'd never intended that people call me names. I only wanted to separate myself from them. "Okay, get on with it," I said.

"I'll bet Amelia gets tired of explaining you," Val said. "Don't you think so?"

"Why should she explain me to anybody?" I said. "I don't explain her."

"You don't have to," Val said. "Can't you see what I mean?"

I could but I didn't want to. "Why are we having

this stupid conversation?'' I asked. I felt like asking her why she seemed to enjoy telling me all this awful stuff.

"I've thought of a way you could have a great time at the dance and surprise everybody."

I stared at her with all the patience I could scrape together. "Why should I?"

"You like a good time, don't you? Everybody does. Think about this. What if you got some horrible clothes. I mean even worse than the ones you usually wear. And what if you showed up at the dance like that?"

I finished my soft drink. "You mean I should dress up like one of the clowns? That's not going to shake anybody up."

"No, no, not like one of the clowns. I mean, what if you looked like a real bag lady. Not with a red nose and crazy wig. I mean, with real rags and shopping bags full of junk."

"Why?" I asked. "I can't see the point of it."

"You'd make the other kids laugh," she said. "And you'd sock it to Amelia for all the times when she's just stood by and let people call you names. And Heather would hate it. She's always hated anything that Amelia hated. They're practically sisters, you know."

She was talking an awful lot, and she was slipping in sentences about Amelia that stung me. Amelia only stood around listening when people called me names? After I'd bashed Warren to get even for her?

And Val was implying something else. "You mean that Amelia's ashamed of me, right?" I asked.

Val shrugged. "The clothes, the trouble at school, being suspended. She must think that you don't know any better. Gee, Erin, I can see why you're doing all this and I accept it—well, your clothes give me a little

103

trouble, but it's a free country. But no way would I let people call you names.''

It didn't occur to me at the time that she obviously had let people call me names—if she'd fought for me, that would have been the first thing she would have told me. No, at that moment, I was hurt and trying to pretend I wasn't—and all the little mean jealous things I'd been trying not to think about Amelia and Heather were growing into big mean things.

If they thought I was Weird Whitney or Bag Lady, then maybe somebody needed to show them how a truly weird bag lady looked. I'd seen a few—and I knew exactly where I could get outfitted for the dance. And wouldn't that embarrass the perfect Whitney cousins!

"Okay, I'll do it," I said.

Val laughed as if I'd just told the best joke in the entire world. I didn't feel very funny—and I couldn't put a name to the odd sensation in the pit of my stomach. But I'd committed myself, and so I got in touch with Nicholas and asked him if he wanted to visit his favorite thrift shop again. I didn't tell him why. We made a date for the next afternoon, and I went off to bed with a book and both of the dogs, determined that I wasn't going to have any regrets for what I was planning to do.

Just before I fell asleep, I remembered that my painting was going to be judged the next day, and I got shivers all over. I wouldn't win, of course.

Or maybe Mrs. Nugent had forgotten to deliver it to the community college campus where the judges were gathering the next afternoon. That would be all right. Then I wouldn't be embarrassed when my painting came in last. Only Mrs. Nugent and Nicholas would ever know. Nobody could laugh at me about that, anyway.

As usual I didn't sleep very well, and when I did, I dreamed of the artist on the waterfront steps. He and I searched crowds for the faces we wanted so much to see—but no one had a face. I ran, ducking between the featureless people, looking for the people I'd lost, but I had no way of knowing if they were there or not.

A cry woke me and I sat up in bed. Amelia was having a nightmare again.

"Oh, don't," she said. "Don't."

I lay back down, determined to let her go on with her bad dream no matter how much it scared her.

But I'd had a few horrible ones myself. So I sat up again and called her name softly until she woke up.

"It was only a dream," I said to her in the dark. "Don't be scared." She mumbled something and went back to sleep.

I stared up at the ceiling and thought to myself that Amelia didn't know what a real nightmare was like. But I knew.

Chapter 13

Sometimes at night I wake up thinking that someone is sitting by my bed. But nobody's ever there—unless it's my shadow, waiting for me to get up so it won't be lonely.

The Castaway

I ended up helping the little guys with a welcome home sign for Heather—not for Heather's sake but for theirs. Cassie and Mimi didn't ask for rescue, but they were having major problems with their first sign. The shelf paper they used had rolled up by itself before the poster paint was dry, so the letters were smeared. And they'd misspelled *welcome*, too.

They had spread the sign out on the living room floor, and were getting all teary over the mess when I walked in on them.

"How about I help you make a new one?" I asked.

"Oh, would you?" Cassie cried, crawling over to hug my knees. "We don't know how to fix this—it just keeps getting worse."

"Let's roll it up and toss it out," I suggested. "There's more shelf paper—we'll do it all over and this time I'll show you how to keep it from rolling back up before you're done."

We used all of the paper and half a roll of masking tape, but by the time we were done, the paper was fastened securely to the hall floor—bare wood was safer than carpet, I explained.

Then I produced a yardstick and a pencil. "Let's plan things out in pencil before we start with the paint."

They didn't see any necessity for that, but I argued my case successfully. Eventually we had penciled letters, all neat and tidy, and *welcome* was spelled right that time.

"Now," I said, handing them each a brush. "Follow the lines and you can't go wrong."

The sign was practically perfect, except for a couple of dog footprints across one end. I turned the footprints into flowers, the little guys were happy, and I felt that I'd made a contribution to the festivities. Heather was arriving on Saturday morning.

On Friday morning at school, Mrs. Nugent showed up at the door of my home room class and beckoned to me. It didn't take any imagination to see that Miss Lear didn't like Mrs. Nugent, because she said, "No interruptions, please," and tried to shut the door in Mrs. Nugent's face.

"This is important," Mrs. Nugent said, her voice all crisp and crinkly like ice. She beckoned to me again, and I joined her in the hall.

"What's wrong?" I asked. My heart was thudding. I must have come in last in the art contest and she was here to break the bad news gently.

"One of the judges called me late last night to give me the results in advance," she said. She grinned the biggest grin I'd ever seen. "They'll be announcing it this afternoon and it will be in tonight's paper. You won. The judge told me it was unanimous."

"I won?" My mouth was so dry I could hardly speak. "Are you sure there wasn't a mistake?"

She shook her head. "No mistake. The one who

called me remembered that you'd won in the grade school division several years ago too. He's impressed with your talent. He said he'd met you once when he was painting at the waterfront."

The artist who had taken me to lunch!

I pulled my hat down as far as it would go and did a little jig. "I can't believe it. I won't believe it yet."

She put one hand on my shoulder. "Believe it. Now, go back to class. Do you want me to stop by the office and have the news announced over the loud speaker?"

"No, no!" I cried. "Please don't do that. I don't want it announced."

She looked at me curiously. "Why not?"

"Nobody will care. Please, just let my family find out first. If it's in the newspaper, then anyone who's interested in that sort of thing will find out and nobody else will have a reason to think about me."

"Oh, Erin," she said. "Come on. This is your day."

I shook my head. "No. Please don't tell."

She shrugged, but I could see that she thought I was crazy. I went back into the class and took my seat.

"Well?" Miss Lear asked. "Why did you see fit to disrupt the class this time?"

My heart was still thudding and my brain seemed to have gone dead.

"Well?" Miss Lear asked.

The machinery in my head finally kicked in. "Were you worried that we were talking about you?" I asked.

Most of the kids in class blurted out laughter and then stopped, probably horrified. Only Nicholas went on snickering.

Miss Lear looked at me for a long, long time, long enough for me to remember that I might not be passing this class—and that I'd been thinking about going to the summer art program at the university.

I looked down at my desk to break eye contact and folded my hands together like a good girl. The moment passed. I heard Nicholas draw a deep breath.

After class, he said, "You won the art contest, didn't you?"

I glared at him. "Don't you dare tell anybody."

"Except my mom," he said. "You want her to know, don't you? Especially since she's one of the people who'll be teaching in the summer art program."

"You're kidding," I said. "Is she? Why didn't you tell me?"

"She just agreed to do it yesterday. And she'd like having you in her class."

I sighed. "My grades are awful. They'll never let me in."

"Your grades probably are awful, but you can say it's because you changed schools. Winning the contest will matter a lot, though. Wait and see."

I hoped he was right. The more unlikely it seemed that I could be in the program, the more I wanted it.

During lunch break, all anybody talked about was Heather. The dance was the following night, and everybody was looking forward to seeing Heather again.

"But I won't be home when she comes," Amelia lamented.

That was news to me. "What? Why not?"

She made a face. "The clowns. Carl booked us for a noon birthday party out of town. We'll have to leave at ten and we won't be back until three, at least. I found out about it this morning."

"Heather will be disappointed," I said. I knew my Fox Crossing cousin was arriving around noon.

"You'll have to make up for me being gone," she said, and she sounded confident that I would.

But I didn't want to do that. Heather and I didn't really know each other anymore. And I wasn't exactly a party girl. The rest of the family would have to do the job.

Lucky Heather. When I arrived at the house that Sunday a few weeks before, no one celebrated. Of course, I wasn't a particularly welcome guest, and one of the reasons was that I'd just been expelled from a school. Funny. I'd been expelled for painting a mural on the wall. Now I'd won a state-wide contest for another painting.

That afternoon Nicholas and I went to the First Pick Thrift Shop again. This time I was looking for something suitable for the dance, and that wasn't so easy.

"If you'd tell me what you want, maybe I could help," Nicholas complained. "You've been through half the bins already."

Mrs. George was watching me curiously. "I know what's in every bin," she said. "Tell me what you're looking for, and if I've got it, I'll drag it out for you."

I decided that I'd better, or I'd be there for a week. "Okay, I need something to wear to a dance. Something that a bag lady would wear if she wanted to look really elegant."

Mrs. George looked at me for a long moment. "I don't imagine they worry too much about looking elegant," she said. "They're having a hard enough time staying alive."

I flinched and felt my face sting as a blush spread over it.

"I didn't mean it exactly that way," I said hastily.

"I know how you meant it," she said. "Kids. You

think it's funny coming in here and getting old clothes so you can pretend that you're homeless and hungry. When you were in here before, I just thought you were another odd little character like Nicholas here, trying to stay independent in a world full of copies. But now I'm not so sure."

I was humiliated. But I was also very defensive. "My cousin works with a troupe of clowns, and they dress in funny old clothes."

"I'm not sure that's so very darned funny, either," Mrs. George said. She waved her hands. "Go on, keep looking until you find what you want. But I charge more for *costumes* than I do for the clothes people need to keep warm."

Eventually I found an old, black velvet skirt with sequins on the hem and a pair of black satin slippers, old-fashioned, but only a little worn at the toes. Nicholas pulled out a black lace blouse with layers and layers of ruffles, each edged with black beads and fake pearls. He was a little subdued. I was ready to cry. The skirt and blouse weren't anything like the outfit Val and I discussed but I was too embarrassed to stay any longer. I paid for the clothes—and Mrs. George was right. She did charge more for costumes. We left the shop silently.

Neither of us spoke until we were a block away. Then Nicholas said, "I never thought about it that way—I mean, that we shouldn't laugh at bag ladies and copy them."

"I never intended copying them!" I said angrily. "At least, not for everyday clothes. I only wanted to copy them for this one time—or at least copy what I thought one of them would wear to a formal dance."

"Maybe, if one were going to a formal dance, she'd want what everybody else had," Nicholas said. He hunched his thin shoulders and stuck his hands in his pockets. "I feel like a jerk," he added.

I sighed. "Yeah."

Now I was totally mixed up. I looked down at my own clothes—a long, gray knit skirt with a long apron over it, one with deep pockets for my drawing material. And a huge, black cardigan with a ratty white lace collar. And my summer hat.

Nicholas was wearing his knickers and a blue sweater with a cartoon figure knitted into the back. And a somewhat smashed straw cowboy hat.

"No bag lady ever looked like us," he said. "We just look weird. Weird is okay. Making fun of people is not."

"Then you think I shouldn't wear this stuff to the dance," I said.

"No bag lady ever looked like that, either," he said. "They've always got layers and layers of clothes so they can keep warm. You're only going to look weirder than usual. But it's the principle of the thing."

I scuffed my high-topped canvas shoes along the sidewalk. "What about the clowns, then?"

He shrugged again and dug his hands deeper into his pockets. "Clowns are always imitating somebody. What about comedians? They do, too. If you think about it, a lot of what we think is funny is making fun of somebody."

"But I don't dress this way to make fun of anybody!" I argued.

"I know. Don't get mad at me. You're just sick of being expected to follow the leader."

"Maybe some of the people who live on the street are sick of following the leader, too," I said.

"Yeah," Nicholas said. "But some of them don't have anyplace else to live."

112

I shook the sack I was carrying. "So what am I supposed to do with this?"

"Beats me," he said. "What were you trying to accomplish?"

"I don't know," I said, but that wasn't true. I wanted to embarrass my cousins. My follow-the-leader cousins.

Stupid. Val got me into this. Why?

"Well, I bought the stuff so I'll find a way to use it," I said.

"Are you going to the dance?" Nicholas asked.

I looked over at him. "Are you?"

"No way," he yelped. "Are you crazy?"

I nodded grimly. "That's how I feel. Somebody sorta talked me into it, though."

"You can change your mind," Nicholas said.

I nodded. "I know."

I got home in time for dinner. As I walked through the living room, I saw the evening paper on the coffee table, still folded and looking unread. Since I was alone in the room, I picked it up and began searching through it. There, in one of the middle sections, on an inside page, I found a small article announcing the winner of the state high school art contest—Erin Elizabeth Whitney. I couldn't help smiling.

But I folded the paper and put it back where I found it, and even though I waited all evening for Aunt Ellen or Uncle Jock or Amelia to discover that small article, no one did.

Tell them, I whispered to myself.

They won't care. Heather was eclipsing everything else. All through dinner and afterward, I heard Heather this and Heather that.

Wonderful Heather was coming for the weekend, Heather who didn't get expelled from school or put on probation. Heather who had a boyfriend.

Heather who had her own family and her own house.

When I went up to the bedroom—Amelia's bedroom—that evening, it seemed jammed with furniture. The folding cot was in the way. There was no room for anything, and it seemed so stupid to have it there.

I went back down and told Uncle Jock that I wanted to move the cot to a corner of the family room. "I'll sleep on it," I said. "I can't stand being in a room that's so crowded."

"Sorry, Erin," Uncle Jock said. "I guess you're right. The cot can go in the family room. But Heather should be the one to use it."

"No," I said. "I want to."

I went back upstairs, and as I did, I heard Aunt Ellen asking Uncle Jock what I'd been talking about. Was I angry? What was wrong? I couldn't make out what his rumbling voice said.

Amelia, of course, was out on a date with Mark, so she didn't know about the new arrangements until she got home that night. I decided that I might as well try out the cot, so by the time Amelia came in, I was tucked into the cot in a corner of the family room, pretending to be asleep.

You can have it all, Heather, I thought. I don't want it.

But I did, I did! I wanted everything she and Amelia had, but there was no way I could get it now. I didn't belong anywhere and I hadn't for a long time.

I rolled over on my stomach and pushed my face into my pillow. *Everything changed when I went to that party when I was ten.*

I hadn't let my thinking run in that direction for a long time. To keep from going crazy, I'd refused to think the awful thoughts. But they were always wait-

114

ing, like books on a shelf growing dusty. But waiting for me to peek inside again.

If I hadn't gone to Patty Murphy's birthday party, my parents would still be alive.

If I'd stayed home, they wouldn't have had any reason to go out in the car that afternoon. And the drunk driver wouldn't have hit them.

I'd have a family and a house and my own dog and cat. My own bedroom. Mine. Not borrowed. My own life, not a borrowed one. I'd have someone to tell about winning the art contest. Someone to go shopping with me to the regular department stores.

I'd be like everybody else.

Chapter 14

I like to watch people I don't know. I don't have
to worry about what might happen to them when
they're out of sight.

The Castaway

On Saturday morning, Heather arrived at eleven
o'clock, an hour early. Amelia had already gone off
with the clowns, Aunt Ellen and the little guys were
doing some last minute shopping, and Uncle Jock had
made a quick run to the bakery to pick up the special
cake for Heather.

I was fixing myself a sandwich to help me last until
lunch—I was so nervous that my stomach was ready
to eat itself—when Heather walked in the front door.
The dogs went crazy, yelping and leaping, and I didn't
get a chance to say anything to her for a long minute.
Then she looked up at me, puzzled, and said, "Erin?
Are you Erin?"

I nodded. I'd have recognized her anywhere. Same
pretty hair, cut in bangs, same bright smile. But I
said, "You must be Heather, right?"

"Yes. Where is everybody? I expected the little
guys to be here, anyway."

"They're shopping. We didn't think you were coming until noon."

"My boyfriend's parents drove me here from Fox
Crossing and they decided to leave earlier than we'd

planned. Will Aunt Ellen and Uncle Jock be back pretty soon?''

"Before noon, that's for sure," I said. "They didn't want to miss your arrival." I was standing there with a knife in one hand and a piece of bread in the other, and suddenly I realized how silly I looked. "I was fixing myself something to eat. Are you hungry?''

She put her suitcase and garment bag down in the living room and pulled off her jacket. "No, not very. I'm too excited.''

I couldn't take my eyes off the garment bag. "Did you bring a long dress for the dance?'' I asked.

"Sure. Want to see it?'' She didn't wait for me to reply, but unzipped the bag and pulled out a pale yellow dress. "Do you like it? I'm going to feel funny going without a date, but Amelia said it would be all right.''

"As long as your boyfriend doesn't mind," I said.

"Oh, he understands," she said. She put the dress back in the bag, looked around, finally opened the hall closet door, and hung the dress there. Then she looked at me. "You haven't changed all that much. I guess I hadn't given it any thought, though, and I was halfway expecting to see the ten-year-old with short hair like mine. And here you are with all that gorgeous hair. It must hang past your waist when it's not braided.''

I nodded.

"You're not as tall as Amelia and I," she said. "But you can sure tell we're all Whitneys. We have green eyes and identical noses.''

I nodded.

"There's a girl in Fox Crossing who's my exact double. Really. You can't tell us apart. When I moved there and saw her for the first time, I thought I was

117

looking in a mirror. We've had lots of fun fooling people."

I nodded again—and felt stupid. I couldn't think of anything to say to her. Finally I mumbled, "How do you like living in a small town, after Seattle?"

"It was hard to get used to," Heather said. "I guess I did have a rough time at first, but mostly because of my stepfather's housekeeper. She hated Mom and me. It was scary sometimes. But by the time my troubles with her were over, I realized that I'd learned to feel at home in the town without noticing it."

"That's nice," I said.

We'd run out of things to say. The silence was awful. I was wondering what to do next when the front door opened again, and in came the little guys and my aunt. Cassie and Mimi went wild over Heather, and my aunt had tears in her eyes. Uncle Jock got home next, and everybody was hugging everybody. I went back to the kitchen and finished making my sandwich, then took it out in the backyard to eat. Nobody came looking for me.

We had lunch an hour later, and I'd ruined my appetite, so I poked my food around my plate and finally excused myself, telling them that I had errands to run that couldn't wait.

I escaped to the park and sat on my favorite bench, thinking all this over while I watched strangers come and go. The sun was warm so I took off my hat, leaned back and closed my eyes.

"Hi, Erin."

It was Jannie, Brady's little sister. She sat down next to me and smiled. A few feet away, Brady stood watching us. He wasn't smiling.

"Brady's taking me to Mary Lou's house," Jannie

said. "She lives on the other side of the park. I'm going to sleep over there tonight."

"That sounds like fun," I told her.

"Brady's going to a dance tonight, and my dad said he could stay home by himself for once."

"I see," I said. I didn't look at Brady.

"Are you going?" Brady asked.

I still wouldn't look at him. "I might," I said.

Did he have a date for the dance? I couldn't bring myself to ask. It wasn't any of my business, anyway.

Jannie supplied the answer. "My dad asked Brady if he wanted to use the car so he could drive his date to the dance, but Brady said, 'What date?' "

"Jannie, for Pete's sake," Brady said. I looked at him then. His face was red.

But Jannie thought her story was worth telling. "So Dad said, 'Why don't you have a date?' and Brady said, 'I forgot to ask anybody.' "

"Why are you going, then?" I blurted.

"I'm on the dance committee," he said. "I have to go."

I got an obscure kind of satisfaction out of that, but I didn't want to examine it very closely.

Jannie wasn't done. "You could dance with him, couldn't you?" she asked me. "Then he wouldn't be all by himself. I hate to be all by myself."

"He won't be," I assured her. Fat chance that Brady Harris would ever be abandoned at a dance.

They left, and I didn't watch them go. The sun went behind a cloud and I left the park, heading in the opposite direction. I had decisions to make, and I couldn't think straight. Was I going to the dance or not? And if I did, was I going to go on with Val's plan? I had the clothes, but I was also uneasy about the idea of showing up dressed to embarrass my cousins. I'd begun to suspect that Val wanted to hurt them

119

for her own satisfaction, not mine, just because they had the fun and friends she wished she had.

It was after two. I still hadn't made plans with Val for being picked up that evening. Maybe she's been trying to call me at home.

I stopped at a pay phone and called Val's house, hoping that she'd be gone. Then my problem would be solved. If I couldn't get hold of her, then clearly I couldn't go to the dance because I wouldn't have a way of getting there. Never mind that I could go with my cousins—I'd already turned down that idea.

Val answered, but she said she couldn't talk—her mother had company and she didn't have any privacy. "Can you meet me somewhere?" she asked. She named the fast-food restaurant she liked.

"Sure," I said. She hung up before I could tell her that I wouldn't be able to spend much time with her. The family would expect me home before dinner, I was certain of that.

Val was late—she was always late—and I was tired of standing outside the restaurant waiting for her. In another minute I'd have left, but Val pulled up then in her mother's car, and hopped out. The weather wasn't all that warm, but Val was dressed for a day at the beach. Everybody at the restaurant stared at us. We represented the two extremes of dressing—she didn't have on enough and I looked like I was ready for January.

We bought soft drinks and dessert, and chose a booth in the back. "Are you ready for tonight?" Val asked.

A sudden feeling of disappointment almost overwhelmed me. I was getting in too deep. I knew it but I couldn't seem to stop it. "I don't know if I want to go or not," I said.

120

"Didn't you and Nicholas go to that place for clothes? Couldn't you find anything?"

"We got an outfit, but I'm not sure it will work. Probably I'll look stupid."

She concentrated on her soft drink for a moment. "I couldn't get a date for you," she said. "I suppose all the guys have been influenced by what the girls say about you."

"Like what?" I asked.

"Oh, you know. I told you before. You don't want to hear it all again. But you could still come with me and my date. That might be better anyway. A guy might get turned off by your act."

"What do you mean, my act?" I asked.

She raised her eyebrows. "You know. The clothes. If you get much worse, the girls will be right. Nobody will want to be seen with you. I could fix you up with some of my things, if you like. Maybe that's the answer."

I shook my head. I definitely didn't think a leather skirt with metal studs in it was an improvement over what I had.

"I don't think I'm going," I said. "I'd probably hate it."

Val smiled. "Heather's here, isn't she? Did she put you down?"

"Of course not," I said. "She's not like that."

Val sighed. "Girls like her don't say things right out. It's the way they look at you. You know. And whisper behind your back. You wouldn't have known about Amelia if I hadn't told you that I'd overheard her."

"You didn't say that Amelia was talking about me. You said that she heard others doing it and didn't object."

"What's the difference?" Val asked. "Me, I'm

loyal to my friends. You wouldn't catch me standing around letting people make fun of you.''

My ice cream was melting but I didn't want it. I shoved the container away. Were Heather and Amelia laughing about me right then? Sitting upstairs in the bedroom with the door shut, poking through my sack of clothes and giggling? Poor stupid Erin. She doesn't know how to dress. She's always in trouble.

I was sick of feeling sorry for myself. ''I'd get the last laugh, all right,'' I said. ''Amelia will probably never speak to me again. She'll think I'm making fun of the clowns, too.''

''Well, that thought had occurred to me.'' Val licked her spoon carefully. ''Who cares? What's so special about them? All they do is dress up in costumes and act like lunatics.''

Two boys came in then, and sat in the booth across from us. Val immediately looked over, smiled, and said, ''Hi. Don't I know you guys?''

''No, but I wish you did,'' one of them said. He glanced at me, blinked, and looked back at Val. ''How you doing?'' he asked her.

A complicated conversation began, made up of half sentences and lots of laughter. And a few hints about taking a ride across town where kids cruised on a beach road.

''I'd have to be home before seven,'' Val said. ''My boyfriend's taking me to a dance tonight.''

The boys looked at each other and grinned. ''Oh, we'll have you back in plenty of time. If you still want to go home, that is.''

Val looked at me then. ''My friend here is going to the dance, too. Whatever she decides is okay with me.''

The boys obviously hadn't planned on taking me

with them, but Val had manipulated them into it. If they wanted Val, they had to take me.

I shook my head. "I don't want to go."

Val kicked my ankle, hard. "Sure you do," she said. "What else are you going to do with a whole, long afternoon? We'd have fun. And they'll get us home in plenty of time." She started laughing suddenly, sounding shrill and stupid. "After all, it's not as if you had to press your dress or anything."

I stood up. "I can't go. Heather's there, and the family's expecting me home. I should have left a long time ago." I started for the door, my face burning.

"Then I'll see you tonight, about eight," Val called out. One of the boys said something and the three of them laughed.

"No, she's fun, she really is," Val said. "We have great times together."

For a moment I was tempted to turn around and go back. But I pushed open the door and stepped out into the street. Overhead, sea gulls drifted on the wind, circling lazily under a gray sky. Two little girls ran past, hand in hand, giggling over something. They reminded me of Cassie and Mimi. Suddenly I was lonely for the little guys.

But Heather and Amelia would be home, too.

Well, I didn't have any place else to go, so I headed for the bus stop.

Riding home, I tried to sort out all the things Val had said. She didn't like my cousins—and they didn't like her, either. Maybe she was my friend. Then again, maybe not. I couldn't tell.

I didn't want to go to the dance. How had I put myself in the position of doing something I didn't want to do? What was stopping me from simply changing my mind?

Resentment bubbled up inside me. If Amelia wasn't

sticking up for me, then she deserved to be embarrassed. And who knew how to embarrass people better than I did?

When I got home, I went in the back door and found Aunt Ellen in the kitchen alone, as I hoped she'd be.

"I'm going to the dance tonight," I told her. "That is, if you don't mind. I've got a ride with a girl from school."

"Don't you want to go with Amelia and Mark? They're taking Heather." Aunt Ellen was busy at the stove, and she didn't look up at me.

"I sorta promised this girl I'd go with her," I said. "She and I don't know too many people, so we'll be company for each other. If I went with Amelia and Heather, they'd end up standing around just to keep me from being alone."

"But do you have a dress?" Aunt Ellen said. "I wish you'd said something sooner. We could have gone shopping, and now there isn't time."

"I've got something that will do just fine," I said.

Aunt Ellen gave me a funny look. "Ah," she said. "Well, all right then."

She was probably wondering what horrible piece of junk I'd come up with. Maybe she was even worried that I might embarrass Amelia and Heather.

Well, Amelia wasn't half as embarrassed as I was, knowing that people were talking about me behind my back.

What did I expect? Haven't they always? When was it ever any different? Annoying my grandparents and everybody else I knew had been sort of a hobby. Annoying them was a lot better than having them feel sorry for me.

Poor old Erin, the orphan. Let's all stare at her and ask her what it feels like.

No, I'd been through all that. Making people angry was better. Then they stayed away and didn't ask questions.

And didn't try to talk about my troubles, the way Brady did. Because what good did talking ever do? It never fixed anything. I was still different from everybody else. Little orphan Erin. Somebody had called me that once in junior high school. Later, when he stole my wallet, I knocked out his tooth. After that I knew that the people who are safe are the ones who are so mean that nobody else wants to tangle with them.

I'd go to the dance and by the time I was through, no one would dare laugh at me again.

Chapter 15

I wonder why some people care so much about other people's private business. Maybe they don't have any private business of their own— they're like empty sacks after all the potato chips are gone.

The Castaway

After dinner the house was as crowded and noisy as an airport terminal. For awhile I thought half the kids in school were there, visiting Heather and catching up on everything that had happened to everyone since Heather had gone away.

Amelia looked happier than I'd seen her since I'd moved in. Having Heather there distracted everybody from the trouble Amelia had earlier in the year. The kids who'd acted awkward around her at school loosened up now that her cousin was back. I suppose everybody was anxious to forget that Amelia had been attacked and humiliated by that rotten Warren Carey. But I hoped that Amelia would remember who her real friends were. Not everyone had supported her.

Heather knew that. I could tell from the way she treated some people that she wasn't forgetting who hadn't wanted to be involved in Amelia's troubles. Heather smiled at them, all right, but she was a little reserved, a little cool. And she turned away from them a little too soon, leaving them anxious.

Amelia saved her warmest smiles for Wendy and Meg. And Heather, of course. It didn't take a genius to see who was in and who was out.

I thought it was a pretty good way of handling things, except that I was out, too. More than just out. I wasn't even in the same universe with my Ideal Teenager cousins.

The crowd left. Heather and Amelia dressed in Amelia's bedroom, with lots of interruptions from phone calls. Heather's mother and stepsister called, and when they were through talking to Heather, they talked to Amelia, then Aunt Ellen, then the little guys, then Aunt Ellen again.

Aunt Ellen held out the phone to me as I passed through the hall. "Do you want to say hello?" she asked.

"No, thanks," I said, and I hurried away so that she wouldn't have a chance to argue.

Flowers had been delivered for my cousins that afternoon, one box from Mark for Amelia and the other from Heather's boyfriend in Fox Crossing. Aunt Ellen helped them fasten the flowers to their dresses. Mark came back, and everybody ran outside to wave goodbye to the girls in their long, gorgeous dresses.

I went upstairs, changed into my new clothes and didn't bother looking into a mirror. My old duster covered me up from neck to ankles, so I'd be able to get out the door without Aunt Ellen seeing what I was wearing. I sat down on the bed I'd been using in Amelia's room and waited for Val to show up.

The room was cluttered with stuff. Heather's clothes were scattered all over, and her cosmetics lay in a heap on the dresser. She'd brought snapshots of her house in Fox Crossing, and her stepfather and stepsister. And her big black dog. The snapshots were strewn on the bed but I didn't pick them up—I didn't touch anything of hers. I didn't even want to look, but I couldn't help it. One of the photos showed Heather and a girl who looked just like her, except that her bangs were swept back. That must have been the friend she'd told me about. And before I looked away, I saw a photo of a boy smiling into the camera.

Where was Val? She was late again, which didn't surprise me. Should I go down and call? I paced around the room for awhile, then pulled a book out of the bookcase and tried to read.

Aunt Ellen knocked on the door. "Are you dressing, Erin?"

"Yes," I said. "I'll be down pretty soon."

"Is your friend going to be late?"

"It looks that way," I said.

Aunt Ellen went away, leaving me to hope that Val wouldn't come to the door when she finally showed up. Aunt Ellen would hate learning that I was going to the dance with her. I should have told Val to honk when she and her date arrived.

I leaned on Amelia's windowsill and looked down at the street. Finally Val got there—in her mother's car. Maybe her date didn't have one. I didn't waste time speculating, but ran downstairs calling out my good-byes as I went.

"Have a good time," Uncle Jock shouted from the kitchen.

"Let's see what you're wearing!" Cassie cried— but I was out the door by then and I closed it behind me quickly. I didn't want anyone in the family to see my clothes.

I got in the front seat of the car because there was no one in it except Val. She took off with a screech of tires, and she looked furious.

"Where's your date?" I asked.

"I wasn't home when he got there, so he left without me," she said. Her face was scarlet with anger and her driving made me nervous.

"How long ago did you get home?" I asked.

"What difference does that make?" she responded. "He should have waited. But my dumb mother told him that I'd been gone all day and she didn't know when I'd be back, so he took off. I can't believe that he stood me up."

"He probably thought you were standing him up," I said, trying to calm her down before she crashed the car. "Maybe he'll be at the dance."

"Well, I'm not speaking to him if he is."

So both of us were going dateless, I thought. "Why don't we do something else tonight?" I asked.

"No way," Val said. "I'm going to dance until my feet fall off." She glanced over at me. "Hey, there'll be guys there without dates. And guys with dates who like to circulate." She reached out and flipped back the corner of my duster. "I can't tell what your clothes look like," she said. "But I didn't forget the rest of our plan. I brought a couple of old paper shopping bags full of junk—they're in the back seat. Carry them in with you and don't put them down. Sorta stand around the edge of the dance floor and look crazy. I'm counting on you to teach your stuck-up cousins a lesson. Do you know what I mean?"

I didn't answer. I knew what she meant and wished I didn't. I looked into the back seat and saw the shopping bags. One had what looked like the leg of an old pair of long johns hanging out of it. She'd gone too far. Or maybe I was feeling guilty after what Mrs. George had said about bag ladies.

"Where's your hat?" Val asked, suddenly.

"It didn't go with the rest of the outfit," I said.

"Hmm," she said. "I wish you'd cut your hair. It

doesn't go with your clothes, either. You never see bag ladies with long hair like that.''

''I'm not going to cut my hair.''

She shrugged. ''I don't care whether you do or not. But everybody else thinks you look like a witch.''

I digested that. ''Fine,'' I said after a moment. I pulled my braid over my shoulder and took off the elastic. ''Now, I'll really look like a witch.'' I loosened my hair. It covered my shoulders and chest, and hung in my lap.

Val didn't look too happy. ''I don't know how you stand it like that.''

''I stand it just fine,'' I said. ''Hey, whose side are you on?''

She laughed suddenly, shrilly. ''Yours—and mine.''

We'd reached the recreation hall, and Val found a parking place at the far end of the lot. We could hear music—the dance had started an hour before.

''Don't forget the shopping bags,'' Val said as she hopped out of the car.

I got a good look at Val for the first time since she'd picked me up. Her dress didn't have a back. It didn't have much of a front, either. And it was soiled.

I was hating this. The closer we got to the entrance, the more I hated the whole idea. When Val handed our tickets to the boy at the door, I wanted to turn and run.

The boy looked at my hair and smiled. Then he looked at my duster and his expression changed. ''Oh, it's you,'' he said. ''Amelia's cousin.''

He was acting as if he'd expected me to show up looking exactly like I did. And with Val. Her plan wasn't going to work. I wasn't going to shock anybody.

I could see the dance floor from where I stood.

Most of the kids were dancing, but a few stood around the walls, watching. There were more girls than boys.

"Come on," Val said. She hurried ahead of me, her high heels pounding. Her bare back was so bony that she looked half-starved. Together, we were a freak show.

No one noticed us at first. Then Val saw a boy smiling uncertainly at her. She rushed off toward him, calling out his name in her shrill voice, and leaving me standing there, shopping bags in hand, feeling like an idiot. I put the stupid bags down and walked away from them. Mrs. George was right. It wasn't fair to make fun of anyone—even though people were always making fun of me.

I saw Amelia at the same moment she saw me. She stopped dancing and said something to Mark, who turned and looked at me. They both smiled, and Amelia started toward me. I turned and walked away.

Wendy and Meg stood together near the refreshment table. For an instant, I thought they didn't recognize me. Then Wendy said, "Your hair. It's gorgeous. I never saw anything like it."

Someone touched my shoulder. I looked back and saw Brady, wearing a dark blue suit and white shirt. He smiled at me, too. "Let's hang up your coat and dance, Erin," he said, not giving me a chance to refuse.

Before I could protest, he took my duster and hung it on the rack by the door, and then led me out on the floor. I could dance—my grandparents had made me take dancing lessons for two years—but I didn't want to, and even worse, the music was slow now. Brady put his arms around me.

"You can't scare me off, Castaway," he said.

My head jerked up. "You knew I wrote those letters?"

He grinned. "Sure. Who else would call herself that?"

"The letters didn't do much good, did they?"

He shrugged. "Yes and no. Next year the school won't be renewing their contract with the place that's been providing the lunches. You started something there. But I doubt if much will ever be done about the football players. The coach protects them. Maybe the Castaway will have to write a few more letters about cheating on exams."

I shook my head. People were beginning to notice me now. Some were smiling, some were only staring.

Val danced by. "Hey, Brady, where'd you find the bag lady?" she called out, and she twirled away without waiting for an answer.

Brady only grinned down at me again. "It's not going to work, Erin," he said.

"What isn't?"

"The act. I don't know who you wanted to shake up, but everybody's used to you by now. And tonight your clothes are gorgeous. Different but gorgeous."

Heather, dancing with Meg's steady boyfriend, didn't recognize me for a moment, and then she gaped at me. Meg's boyfriend grinned.

Val came by again. "Where are your shopping bags?" she demanded. "Why are you dancing?" She stopped and stared at my clothes. "Hey, what's going on? You said . . ."

Brady swung me past her. My hair flew out like a cape, swirling around me.

I'd come here to embarrass my cousins, but something else was happening instead, and I wasn't prepared. I pulled free from Brady and ran over to collect my duster.

Amelia caught my arm. "Heather and I want to talk to you for a minute," she said.

"What about?" I asked.

"Your clothes. Come on, have a glass of punch with us."

I tried to read her expression. What were she and Heather going to do, try to fix me up so I'd look better? Take me home and dress me in something of Amelia's, then bring me back all reformed?

"My clothes suit me just fine," I said, and I walked away from her.

Once I was outside I ran toward home. I passed the high school. The small park was ahead of me, dark and still. On impulse, I turned onto the path.

It was so quiet there that I could hear my own heart beat. I sat on my favorite bench. The pond water was still. The air was scented with new grass.

"Erin?"

I recognized Brady's voice calling me. He was trotting down the path, and I could barely see him in the dark.

"Let me alone," I said.

"Not this time," he said as he sat down beside me. "Not this time."

Chapter 16

Sometimes the nicest thing you can say about
life is that it feels like a paper cut, but there are
a few people around who can take out the sting.
                                              The Castaway

Brady leaned back on the bench and I gritted my
teeth, waiting for the lecture to start.

"We sure had some good times here," he said.
"Remember feeding the squirrels? We could bring
them something tomorrow."

"I'm busy tomorrow," I barked. "I'm always
busy."

He was silent for a moment. "Maybe you could
try to make room for a friend."

"I've got plenty of friends and I don't need you."

He didn't speak again for a long time. I was getting
cold, but I wouldn't have admitted it if my life de-
pended on it.

"I've missed you," he said at last. "A lot."

Suddenly the hard knot I had in my throat dissolved
and I began crying—about everything—my folks and
Brady's mother and because I'd tried to hurt my cousins. Every rotten thing I'd ever done weighed me
down like stones.

Brady slid his arm around my shoulders. "Sometimes I've wanted to cry about you. But you've made
me laugh the way nobody else ever has. Those letters

134

to the school paper. And that awful prison farm sweater. And your hat. We've had some good times, Erin, even if you never wanted to admit it."

It was true. The best times since I'd come back to Seattle were the times I'd spent with him. He'd understood me, even better than Nicholas.

I threw both my arms around him. "I miss the way you made me feel."

We sat there like that without talking. Then Brady said, "I think you miss the way everybody made you feel."

"Feeling hurts."

"Sometimes," he said.

"I didn't want to feel anything after my parents died."

"I know."

I tightened my grip on him, afraid that he'd get up and leave. I must have been half-strangling him, but he didn't complain. And I was getting the shoulder of his nice suit all wet from my tears.

"If you stay by yourself, you don't get hurt so often," I said. "If you start caring about somebody, then something happens and you don't have them anymore."

He didn't say anything.

I sighed. "I wanted people to notice me, but from a distance. I didn't mind if they laughed, just so they didn't get too close."

"Didn't work, though, did it?" he asked. "Here I am."

"I don't know why."

He wrapped my hair around one of his hands and rubbed it against his face. "I get such a kick out of your clothes. I wait to see you at school in the morning to find out what new outfit you've put together. And you've got his funny little scowl—you always look like you're only a split second away from laughing and you're trying not to. You're different and

135

funny and smart and talented. Why wouldn't I want to be close to you?''

''Nobody else does.''

''How would you know? You never look around to see.''

I pushed Brady away. ''Are you feeling sorry for me?''

''I'm sorry that your parents died,'' he said quietly. ''I'm sorry my mother died, too. People are supposed to feel that way. It's okay. It's also okay to let other people tell you how bad they feel because something awful happened to you.''

''I don't think I can change,'' I said.

He laughed a little. ''Who wants you to change? Do you want Nicholas to change? He's his own self.'' Brady shook his head. ''Boy, is he! And you're yourself, clothes and all. I'm not talking about the outside of you. I'm talking about the inside, the part you've kept locked up for so long that you don't have real feelings anymore. At least, not any happy ones.''

''How do you know?'' I demanded.

''Because I felt like that for a long time. All through my mom's illness—she was sick for so long that I hardly remembered when she wasn't, and it scared me. So after a while I just concentrated on school. Getting good grades and doing a lot of volunteer work. I kept busy so I wouldn't have to think. And afterward, I worked even harder. I wouldn't let myself look back.''

''I know how that is,'' I said.

He put his arm around me again. ''Yes. But I don't have your sense of humor, so funny clothes and a crazy old hat never occurred to me. I made sure in other ways that nobody could really catch up with me, though.''

''But you're one of the most popular boys in school,'' I said. ''You must know that. Everybody thinks you're wonderful.''

"But nobody knew that I used to dread talking to people for fear they'd say they were sorry about my mother. I didn't want to be reminded."

"Yes," I said, recognizing the feeling. "That's how it is."

"Things weren't so hard for me as they were for you, though," he went on. "I had my dad and Jannie. After a while I realized that I needed to lean on them a little. Then I began feeling better."

But I hadn't had anybody to lean on, not really.

Brady must have read my mind. "You've got all sorts of people to lean on now," he said. "You've got a family—with more cousins than anybody else I know. And you've got goofy little Nicholas. And you've got me if you want me."

I closed my eyes and leaned against him. "Maybe I could think about it," I said. "Maybe I could try."

"Sounds good to me," he said. "Now, come back to the dance with me."

"Looking like this?" I said, standing up so that he'd be reminded of what I was wearing.

"I always thought black was glamorous," he said, and he burst out laughing and swung me around. "Especially black with beads and lace and ruffles." He looked down at me then, soberly. "You're pretty, Erin, even if you never wanted to be."

We went back to the dance, and I didn't know if anyone noticed us or not because he was the only one I looked at. And when he took me home afterward, he kissed me good-night on the front porch.

"Let's go to the zoo tomorrow," he said. "That's where I talked to you first. Let's start all over."

I nodded. "I'll try my best." Then I looked up at him and grinned. "But I'm going to wear my prison farm sweater."

"And the long black skirt with the big pockets," he said. "I like that best."

I was going to go in then, but he stopped me. "By the way," he said, "the school paper will have an article on the front page about your winning the state contest."

"How did you find out?" I asked.

"Nicholas told me first, of course. And then Mrs. Nugent talked to me about it. Like it or not, you'll be famous next week."

I slept without dreaming that night, and in the morning after Amelia and Heather got up, I went through the sack of clothes in Amelia's closet. I pulled out the black skirt Brady liked, and a striped shirt that wasn't too ragged or ridiculous. I picked up the prison farm sweater, then put it back and took out a plain red cardigan instead. It had holes in the elbows, but they weren't too big. Maybe I could make a few concessions to the rest of the world.

From the shelf, I took down the beautiful length of skirt material Mrs. Brown had given me. This was as good a day as any to begin learning to sew.

I showed up at breakfast all dressed but without my hat. No one said anything, but I saw my aunt and uncle smile at each other.

When the meal was over, they took the little guys off to buy plants for the flower beds. I saw Amelia watching me across the table, trying not to grin. My first impulse was to say something rude. Instead, I said, "Is something wrong?"

Amelia began giggling, and then Heather laughed out loud.

I was getting angry. "What's going on?" I demanded.

"We wanted to talk to you last night," Amelia said. "But you and Brady didn't look as though you wanted to be interrupted. Where do you get your clothes?"

Oh, great, I thought. Maybe she was embarrassed last night after all.

"I don't mean what you wore to the dance," Amelia said. "That was fabulous, even if it was old-fashioned. I mean your school clothes. They're the most horrible, hideous, wonderful things I ever saw, and I want some just like that for the clown act. Heather says you have more imagination than I do, and she's right."

I was so surprised that I couldn't talk for a moment so I poured myself another glass of juice. Without looking at anyone, I said, "I've been buying my clothes at a place called First Pick. It's open Sunday afternoons. Brady and I could drop you off on our way to the zoo."

Amelia and Heather exchanged a quick glance. "That sounds good," Amelia said. "We ought to call the other clowns, too. They'll want to be there."

"Or," I said, looking at her innocently, "I could sell my stuff to you for three dollars a pound."

Heather looked startled, but Amelia caught on right away that I wasn't serious about charging her. "That's too much," she argued. "After all, those are used and second-hand both. I won't pay more than a dollar a pound."

I pretended to consider her offer seriously. "Well, I suppose that's all right," I said finally, with a big, fake sigh. "After all, you're my cousin."

"You'd better believe it," Amelia said, and she raised her juice glass. "Here's to us, the Whitney girls."

Heather clinked her glass to Amelia's, and then both of them looked at me. I raised my glass, too.

"All three of us," I said.

JEAN THESMAN was born in Seattle and still lives there with her husband and their dogs. She is the author of several novels for young readers, among them *Couldn't I Start Over?* and *The Last April Dancers*, both available in Avon Flare editions.